AS THE EARTHEN STAG WALKS

BOOK I OF THE SIMULACRUM

DAVID CHESNEY

Jonathan,
Here's to the best
secret santa ever!

David Chesney

1

I ntense heat blasted Seelios's face as he approached the fire of the open furnace. He swept sweaty blond hair out of his eyes and grabbed a shovel. He jabbed it into a pile of shimmering red rocks and leaned into it with all his weight, barely piercing the heap. Rocking back, he hoisted the small load and shoved it into the furnace flames with the grace of a toddler with a broomstick. The sudden flare of the fire made Seelios jump and some of the rocks tumbled out onto the stone floor, scattering dusty red debris that glittered in the light. Already exhausted, Seelios's quivering arms let the shovel drop with a metallic ring.

"It's not enough. The flames need to be stronger," his father said in between swings of his hammer. He was a stocky man with short brown hair and chiseled facial features, tough inside and out. It wasn't easy being the son of the most respected blacksmith in the land, especially when that son seemed to be the apple that fell so far from the tree.

"This metal is unlike anything we've forged. Go fetch someone to help you feed the fire faster," the blacksmith said and continued to ring the anvil with heavy strokes of precision.

Seelios felt a pang of shame. He'd been helping his father for the better half of the day yet, despite his best efforts, couldn't keep up the required pace.

It didn't help that Seelios inherited none of his father's strength. Villagers questioned their blood relationship, relenting only after looking into their eyes. Seelios and his father shared the same striking, silver eyes that glimmered in the sunlight, a feature that no one else in Fembleton had ever seen. That, however, was where the similarities ended. Seelios had thick blond hair and limbs as thin as a child's, despite him being a young man late into his teenage years. He was of little use as a smith's apprentice, barely able to lift even the lightest of tools.

When Seelios was younger, he was given the choice of working on one of the village farms or helping in the forge. Wanting to be able to spend time with his father, the latter was his obvious choice. He often questioned whether his father felt the same.

Seelios took off his apron and set it on the work table before rushing to the door. He stopped when he heard the hammering go quiet. He turned and saw his father hold up a long, thin band of metal for inspection. It glowed with a fading red hue from the heat of the furnace and resonated with an unseen force. It quickly cooled, and the surface changed to a brilliant rippling bronze and gold.

His father caught him staring and smiled. "Orichalcum, the metal of the gods." He held it out, gripped with a long pair of tongs. "The most useful metal known. Stronger than tempered steel, it can hold an edge forever if made into a blade. One day, when you're ready, I'll show you how to forge it."

The shining metal's pattern was mesmerizing, but it wasn't the first time Seelios had seen it.

While his father was away, Seelios and his friend, Garrick, found a secret cache in the wall of the forge years before. Carefully hidden behind a heavy shelf, it was a space just big enough for a small weapons rack that held fine crafted swords, daggers, and other dangerous looking weapons that Seelios didn't recognize; however, none of the weapons compared to the beauty of the spear that lay in the center. The shaft seemed to be made of a silver so brilliant it looked like a star shining in the middle of the night. The bladed tip gleamed like fire, its metal surface swirling with unique patterns of gold and bronze. If Seelios's father knew that he even looked in that cache he surely would've been punished, so he kept his mouth shut.

His father thrust the orichalcum into a water basin and it hissed, releasing a cloud of steam. He turned to Seelios with a serious face. "A metal of this caliber requires a precise process, one that requires a constant feed of fire rock to keep the flames hot." He frowned at the heap of shiny red rocks against the far stone wall. It was much less than half of what they started the day with.

"Go now, quickly. With all the work we have left, we don't have much more to spare. This must be finished well before I leave for Gorynn Monastery." his father said.

Seelios nodded. "Yes, Father." He wiped the collection of soot and sweat from his forehead as he pulled open the door to reveal the sunlit landscape of their small lakeside village. His skin cooled to the touch of the fresh air.

Their forge was surrounded by blighted farmland filled with stalks of shriveled vegetation, swaying in a breeze the rolled off the distant Southern Mountains. It had been a few weeks since the mysterious decay, but

Seelios still wasn't used to the sight of the unhealthy crops. There was concern among the villagers, but no one knew what to do.

When he stepped out and closed the door behind him, Seelios could hear the bustle of Fembleton's market. The noise came from beyond the strip of shriveled crops that separated the forge from a gathering of stone and timber shops that made up the heart of town. Their pointed roofs fit in with the surrounding pine trees and mountain peaks in the background. He turned and looked across the river, behind the forge, to the farmland estates where Garrick lived. Seelios and Garrick had been friends for a long time and if there was anyone he could count on to help him with the furnace, it was him.

A man well into adulthood, Garrick had a troubled mind and a difficult past. He's had no family since he was a child and struggled in everyday relationships with people, yet found friendship in Seelios. Having a distant father and a non-existent mother, Seelios found common ground with Garrick.

Garrick was likely working in his fields across the river while the sun was still high.

Seelios ran toward the stone bridge that crossed over the Brascella River that flowed out of the sparkling waters of Fembleton's lake. The dark green shades of the forest accentuating the distant shore were dwarfed by a backdrop of the snow-capped Southern Mountains that reflected majestically on the lake's surface.

Seelios rounded one of the stone pylons that framed both sides of the bridge. The rushing current of the river could be heard underfoot as it ran in between the rusty metal bars of the lake gate that kept boats, and sometimes people, from getting swept down river. Refreshing mist sprayed over his face, a welcome sensation after a day laboring in front of a furnace.

Despite Fembleton's small size, it saw many visitors not only because of its lake, but also for its location on one the most highly used routes on the continent: the Trade Road.

Seelios crossed over the bridge and into the farmlands that served as Fembleton's primary food source, a good portion of which was owned by Garrick. The fields stretched for at least half a mile before it ran into the surrounding forest. As Seelios moved along the dirt road he noticed the state of the crops only seemed to worsen the further he got from the river. His lungs choked on the strong odor as he took deep breaths during his run. It was a time of peril for the villagers of Fembleton, and some folks had even considered leaving in search of more fertile grounds. Word from passing travelers seemed to suggest that this town was the only place that suffered from the blight.

The fields were mostly empty, to Seelios's surprise. Farmers were usually found milling about with horses or cattle, tending to the land. Perhaps they gave up on the crops, deeming it a lost cause. Seelios called out Garrick's name, but there was no response.

Garrick's house stood in the middle of his farmland estate, between his large stables and towering stone granaries. The house itself was large by Fembleton's standards, having multiple levels with ample living space and several bedrooms. Its first floor was composed of stone that served a solid foundation for the timber frame that stretched up to white-washed walls and wood roofs that arched over windows. While Garrick was modest, it was clear that he inherited a wealth far greater than what anyone else had in Fembleton.

Seelios pounded on the iron banded wooden door.

Because of the manor's size, a soft knock couldn't be heard if Garrick was in his study or bedroom. Seelios pulled his arm back for another attempt when he heard footsteps echoing down the stone hallway. The door opened and the manor's caretaker appeared.

"Ah, Master Strongheart. A pleasure to see you," the caretaker said with a smile. He grimaced and waved a hand in front of his nose. "Gods be good, it seems to only be getting worse."

Seelios turned and frowned at the rotting crops behind him, nodding in agreement. "Father says its unlike anything he's ever seen here before."

"Indeed. I do hope it passes soon." The caretaker's face turned to a gentle smile as he looked back down at Seelios. "How can I help you?" He was an elderly man with a wrinkled face that had lines of laughter. Those lines were signs of a past self that had become replaced with solemn expression. The Sandwin household has experienced little joy since Garrick's parents were killed.

"I was hoping to find Garrick. I'm in need of his help."

The caretaker frowned. "I'm afraid I haven't seen him all day. Not in the fields?"

Seelios shook his head. "If you don't mind, I'll try the library."

"Please, go right ahead. With how often you use it it's practically yours."

Seelios thanked the caretaker. The Sandwin Library was a curiosity to the villagers when first built. Its stone walls and cathedral architecture led everyone to believe it housed treasure, but were disappointed to learn that it had nothing but bindings of paper with ink scribbled over them. Seelios, however, knew there was something truly remarkable in that library. He knew the true value of books and would spend every waking moment browsing the Sandwin shelves if he could.

There was an entrance from inside the manor, but Seelios didn't want to dirty the caretaker's cleaning with soot and filth from the forge. When Seelios arrived at the library's smaller, but still ornate wooden door, he gave another knock. No answer came from inside, so he creaked the door open and revealed a room of near total darkness. Streams of light from towering windows pierced through the shadows, brightening specks of dust that danced through the air.

"Garrick? Are you in here?" Seelios called out. His voice echoed off stacks of books on shelves that stretched to the ceiling. He sighed, resigning himself to the realization that he'd have to look in the one place he hoped not to find Garrick: the tavern.

2

F   embleton's tavern and inn was located in the outskirts of the market square, one of the first buildings seen when travelers took the path into town from the Trade Road. Seelios ran back through the Sandwin farmlands toward the bridge. With so much time already exhausted he hoped the search would end soon. His father would be expecting him back at any moment.

Seelios almost slipped on the wet planks with his reckless pace as he crossed the bridge. Packed dirt underfoot turned to cobbled stone as he entered Fembleton's square. The crowd was thinner than usual, gathered around the few carts and wagons that had set up their wares on display. Merchants were selling fruits, dried meats, leather goods, and there was the occasional trinket dealer hoping to lure a superstitious traveler into a sale. Fembleton's farmers normally occupied many of the stalls, selling crops and farm goods by the arm-load, but those shelves and tables sat deserted. No traveler would buy wheat or corn that smelled of festering swamp water.

Fembleton's ornery baker stepped out of his shop and

yelled at Seelios to slow down. Seelios gave a smile and waved as he rounded the corner of the bakery and sprinted through the crowd. Villagers stepped out of the way and threw annoyed looks. He slowed to a walk as he reached the edge of the square, cobbled stone turning back to dirt road. The two-storied Withertree Tavern and Inn stood beside him, there to welcome weary travelers who couldn't make it another step. Lanterns hung around the oak door and a swinging wood painted sign jutted out from one of the beams.

Seelios bent over while taking deep breaths, his lungs burning from the short run. It was early in his life when he realized he was different than most. A village as small as Fembleton provided him little opportunity to interact with children of his age, but folks were quick to let him know that he wasn't growing as a boy should be. He was tall enough, but weak. He struggled to lift and push most things that came easy to others. His father assured him there was no reason to be ashamed, but Seelios felt otherwise. There was a difference between being different and not belonging. Garrick was one of the few people in town who treated him like a normal person.

Seelios lifted his head and adjusted the tunic that hung loosely on his frame. The dirt path stretched out before him, running along the river to merge with the Trade Road. If he kept going he'd eventually be led to Paloise, the City of Light, a fortified capital where the God of Light supposedly dwelled. All lands within Paloise's kingdom were under the God of Light's protection, which included Fembleton. There'd never been any need for a deity's intervention in Fembleton, but it still made villagers uneasy that the God of Light hadn't been seen in years, decades even. In his stead he empowered a handful of people with divine strength, but they were never seen far from the Paloise walls. Villagers dreaded the day that they get attacked by anything more threatening than a pack of hungry wolves.

Seelios dusted off his pants and tunic as best he could before entering the tavern. He took a deep breath in preparation, already hearing the muffled commotion of a lively crowd through the windows and walls. He pulled open the front door, revealing a loud scene of drunken debauchery that near overwhelmed his senses.

The tavern was a simple room with several circular wooden tables and a wide bar in the back. The walls were mounted the heads of various hunted animals. Behind the bar were two crisscrossing long swords, most likely forged by Seelios's father.

It was surprisingly busy for the middle of the day. The patrons inside seemed to be noisy and alive, but the sense of merriment was lost on them. The crowd at the bar seemed agitated. Garrick was sitting alone on a stool and had a bit of a sway to his posture. He was a brawny man with a handsome face, often drawing the attention of the village maidens. His tunic and pants were smudged with dirt, likely from farm work earlier in the day. It was a bit uncharacteristic of him to be seen in town in such a disorderly and unkempt state.

Glad to avoid the riled drunks of the town, Seelios made his way over to his solitary friend. He had only taken few steps when someone at a nearby table waved a full mug of ale dangerously close to Seelios's face, cascading some of the brew onto the floor. He flinched and took a step back. The local butcher pulled the mug back and turned his head, eyes glazed and struggling to stay open.

"Aye, sorry about that lad," the butcher said with a jolly face. He shifted his heavy figure and the back of his chair creaked against his drunken lean. "Was just telling my friends here a bit of a tale and got too excited."

Seelios nodded and gave a shy smile before continuing through the maze of tables filled with travelers and locals.

"No children in the— Oh, come on in, Seelios," Emeline, the bar keep, said over the clamor of patrons. She was easily one of the prettiest women in the village with vibrant red hair that tumbled down over her emerald green dress and eyes as blue as a crisp clear day.

Seelios gave her a wave and approached the bar. He noticed a figure he didn't recognize, sitting in the shadow of a corner close to Garrick. It looked like a man, but part of his face was concealed by the hood of his dark-brown cloak. He sat at his table, no food nor drink, surveying the scene with a single expressionless eye that peered out from between the folds of fabric.

Seelios eyed the cloaked man with a wary look as he eased into the stool next to Garrick.

"Thought I'd find you here. Who's he?" Seelios said in a hushed whisper. "Leaves me a little unsettled."

Garrick shrugged and said, "Ask him yourself," as he continued to stare straight ahead.

"Be with you boys in just a moment," Emeline hollered from the other side of the bar. She flashed a smile that could warm the hearts of even the weariest of souls. Several patrons drew annoyed looks at her as they waved their empty mugs impatiently.

Garrick brightened with a smile at Emeline, but returned to his sour face when she turned away. He strummed his fingers beside his half-finished ale. Seelios arched an eyebrow at his friend. He was a solemn fellow, but he usually showed at least a tiny bit of enthusiasm when they greeted each other.

"Something troubling you?" Seelios asked. "Is it the crops? I saw them earlier, they've become worse."

Garrick flicked his eyes to Seelios, then down to his mug. He gave a heavy sigh with an expression that transitioned to concern.

"If you were anyone else I'd be hesitant to share," Garrick said, still looking down. "But I know I can trust you."

Seelios nodded with a serious expression. "What is it?"

Garrick lifted his head after a moment and pursed his lips. "Strange nightmares have been haunting me as of late."

Seelios gave a small frown. "That's nothing to be ashamed of."

Garrick shook his head. "You don't understand." Garrick squinted in concentration, as if he were working to recall the memory. "It's cold and dark. I know nothing of where I am. I don't know if I'm anywhere. But there's . . . a voice. It hisses from the darkness, saying terrible things. Whatever it is, whomever it belongs to, it's sinister."

Garrick took a sip from his ale and set the mug back down on the bar. He turned to face Seelios and leaned on the bar with one arm. "When it speaks, it tells me to do unspeakable things. Hateful things," Garrick said in a hushed voice. "It told me to kill your father."

Seelios saw the skin on his friend's arm prick up and turn to gooseflesh. He saw the nervous look in Garrick's eye, one of concern and fear. Garrick took a sip of his mug and they sat in silence while the banter of the tavern continued in the background.

"What do you think it means? What of your parents?" Seelios asked.

Garrick gave a sigh and rolled his eyes away. "I know where your head is leading, Seelios. I'm a grown man. I need no lecturing from a kid." The drunken slur was becoming apparent.

Garrick rarely brought up their age difference, but the few times he did it always put a hurtful distance between them. The last time it happened they didn't speak for the span of a week.

"You rarely talk of it. It's helpful to get things off your chest," Seelios said.

"I said piss off!" Garrick yelled, sending bits of spit that landed on Seelios.

Nearby folks hushed their conversation and turned toward Garrick.

"Sorry. Was only trying to help," Seelios said in a hurt tone. He slid off the bar stool. "I needed your help at the forge, but I'll manage."

Seelios started walking away, but Garrick reached out and grabbed his arm. His hand felt massive around Seelios's tiny limb.

"Wait. I'm the one who should be sorry," Garrick said. "I can't explain what's happening to me. I'm scared." Garrick dropped his grip. "What if these nightmares do have meaning? What if . . . what if it's a different side of me?"

Seelios felt confused. He wasn't sure what Garrick was talking about.

"Is there something else you want to tell me?" Seelios asked as he slid back onto the stool.

Garrick grew silent and lowered his gaze again. "In my nightmare I feel anger and hate. And more times than I'd like to admit, those feelings have come while I'm awake."

Seelios took in a sharp breath. "Have you done something?"

Garrick barely shook his head from side to side with a distant look that seemed as if his mind were miles away. "It's just, strange things are happening. The blight, I think it's coming from . . . ." He drifted off into silence. He turned back to Seelios with a look of hesitance, like he wanted to ask something, but wasn't sure how.

"Have you noticed anything strange about the Daylight Star?" Garrick asked.

Seelios was taken aback by the question. The Daylight Star was a light in the sky so bright that it sparkled like a diamond among the clouds. The light, however, was barely visible during the night when most stars could be seen in full radiance. Some people thought it wasn't a star at all, but one of the gods high in the heavens, watching over them with its protecting gaze. Some of those same people said that's where the God of Light disappeared to, even though the Daylight Star twinkled in the sky long before he went missing.

"Nothing strange I can think of," Seelios said. He scratched his blond hair. "What of it?"

"Never mind," Garrick said with a dismissive wave of his hand.

Garrick lifted his eyes and stared at Emeline over the bar. He watched as she moved between eager men waving their hands to get her attention, her long red hair flipping back and forth.

Seelios noticed a faint smile spread across Garrick's lips as he stared.

"She's the reason why I'm here," Garrick said. "She drives those feelings away."

Garrick finished the rest of his ale. "I'm going to tell her how I feel. I'm ready."

Alarm flashed across Seelios's face. "What? No, Garrick, not like this. You're drunk."

Garrick's expression turned to annoyance, and he faced

Seelios. Thinking Garrick was about to have another angry outburst, Seelios grabbed the bar to push himself away.

Garrick's eyes widened as it locked onto the ring on Seelios's hand. "That's it. You're the key! You can tell me if I'm good enough for her."

Seelios raised his eyebrow in curiosity, then lit up with horrible realization. "No. We talked about this." Seelios's hand went to his left index finger where the simple stone band was.

Garrick pointed at the ring. "It has the power. It can tell me." He threw a gaze up into the air in an exaggerated motion, throwing his other hand out in a wide arc. "Truly, to not think of this before is embarrassing," Garrick said.

"We can't. I can't. My father forbids it. We shouldn't even be speaking of it," Seelios said.

Garrick grabbed two fistfuls of Seelios's dirty tunic. The stench of alcohol was heavy on Garrick's breath.

"Please, Seelios. These nightmares tear me apart. I need this." Garrick sat back down on the stool and hung his head. "I just need proof of who I am."

Seelios could tell his friend was struggling, his suffering palpable. There were few times that Seelios felt like he could actually help Garrick with anything. Another opportunity might not come along for quite some time.

Seelios slid the ring off his finger with reluctance. "Fine. But no one can see," he whispered as he glanced to his side out of the corner of his eye. Garrick's face brightened and he edged forward.

Seelios knew the ring held power the moment his father gave it to him and, much to his father's surprise, learned to use the power at quite the young age. It took much convincing to allow Seelios to wear it in public, with the adamant condition that he not use it in front of anyone.

Seelios stared down at the circle of stone in his palm, face to face with the promise that he was about to break. He looked up at Garrick, who stood from his stool.

Seelios gave a heavy sigh and closed his eyes to concentrate, focusing on the weight of the small piece of jewelry in his hand. He tried to block out all the distractions in the bar. The shouting. The banging of drink ware. The scraping of wood as people shuffled in and out of seats. In the blank of his mind, the circle sat suspended on his palm. It began to give off heat, a tender warmth that felt soothing and familiar. Slowly, glowing yellow runes of indecipherable meaning began to appear on the outside of the band. One was an eye with angled lines in symmetrical frame. Others bore shapes of dots and swirls crafted into mysterious glyphs. They looked tribal and ancient, containing tales of power and the creation of all things.

The first time Seelios saw those runes appear he nearly burst from excitement. The ring came to life and communicated with Seelios in a way that connected directly with his mind. It didn't speak words, at least those that he could understand, but drew emotions and vague understandings of knowledge. The first time he activated the runes he suspected that it might be a fabled runic artifact, a legendary object forged by one of the gods.

Ever since Seelios first learned of runic artifacts as a child, he dreamed of seeing one with his own eyes. In fact, it was practically the dream of every mortal to hold an object that could unleash godly powers. Seelios would play with sticks, stones, smithing tools, and whatever else he could find, pretending to be a great hero dashing around and saving damsels from demons. Most runic artifacts were said to look like ordinary objects unless they were activated, making it easy for a child's imagination to run wild.

Seelios watched with his mind as the glowing runes hung suspended, beckoning his call. His body may have been standing in a tavern, but his mind was elsewhere with the ring.

Garrick's voice came like a distant shout, as if he was across the Ernus ocean. His cries became increasingly louder, causing Seelios's attention to break away from the ring.

"Seelios!" Garrick yelled as he shook Seelios's shoulder.

Seelios opened his eyes and Garrick was huddled beside him, his other hand covering the ring in Seelios's open palm. Blinking, Seelios looked at Garrick. "What's wrong? I was almost finished—"

Someone stood behind Garrick. The figure in the brown traveler's cloak had moved away from the corner. One exposed eye was open wide with curiosity, yet his face seemed plain and expressionless.

Garrick turned toward the man, taking a step. "You best be walking along if you know what's good for you."

The man's eye darted up to Garrick, to Seelios, then down to Seelios's outstretched hand. Seelios realized he still held the ring in his open palm. The runes had nearly faded from view, but small bits of glowing light were still left. He shoved the ring into a pocket.

The man's eye remained wide as he looked from the pocket up to Seelios's face. Garrick took another step toward him, bringing them so close they could almost kiss.

The man looked up at Garrick for a moment, then rushed away in a hurried shuffle that made him look like he struggled to bend his knees. He moved his arms in small jerks as he did an awkward rocking motion that carried him toward the tavern's front door. Halfway across the floor he turned his head to look back toward Seelios and Garrick, unaware of the butcher who was waving his mug around in jovial animation.

The mug knocked into the shoulder of the wide-eyed man. He jumped back and flailed about like a frightened kitten, raising his arm in defense, but it did little to block the shower of ale that soaked his entire arm and much of his cloak.

"Aye, there lad. A thousand apologies!" the butcher said as he leapt out of his chair. His plump cheeks were flushed red from the alcohol. "Let me buy you a—"

The ale soaked man clamored the rest of the way out the door. The motion was so chaotic that he nearly ran into the door frame, having to brace himself with his hand to keep himself from crashing into it.

The butcher stood, dumbfounded at the man's behavior, as he watched him retreat out the swinging door. He gave a shrug and settled his large belly back into his seat. The men with him had a jolly laugh, pointing and mocking at the butcher's expense.

"He smelled strange," Garrick said as he looked toward the door.

"What do you mean?" Seelios asked.

Garrick wrinkled his forehead. "He smelled like dirt. Not like a farmer after working the field, but like the field itself."

"What was that whole mess about?" Emeline stood next to them on the other side of the bar, staring with sparkling blue eyes. Her ruby-red hair framed her perfect face.

Garrick stared at her, blinking for a moment. "H—hi, Emeline." He shifted nervously on his feet.

She looked at him with confusion, then smiled again. "Hi, Garrick. Hope that fellow didn't bother you boys too much, never seen him before." She looked at the entrance with a small frown before turning back and picking up Garrick's nearly empty mug. "How about another?"

Garrick gawked at her. His lips moved, but nothing came out.

Emeline looked to Seelios. "Is Garrick ill?"

Seelios watched his friend struggle with the task he was so defiant about but moments ago. Seelios nudged Garrick. "Well?"

A long silence passed between the three of them while Emeline waited for Garrick to spit something out. He turned to Seelios, wide-eyed, then back to Emeline.

"Emeline," he said. He cleared his throat and took a deep breath. "There's something I've wanted—"

The door to the kitchen burst open behind Emeline and the owner of the Withertree, Cassius, came out holding an empty travel sack. It was with a certain sense of irony that the prettiest in town worked for the ugliest. Cassius was a balding elderly man with liver spots all over his head and face. Long, stringy white hair dangled from the sides of his head to his shoulders. His beady eyes held no warmth, and when he smiled a crooked set of brown teeth sent shivers through anyone unlucky enough to witness it. He was wearing a pale yellow tunic that looked as if it was put on with haste, still crinkled about his bony shoulders and chest.

"Damnit, woman, if I catch you idly standing about again you'll be cleaning my stables!" Cassius spat.

Emeline threw Cassius a seething gaze and moved back toward the men waiting on the other side of the bar. Cassius followed her with his glare. His ugly appearance added to the expression of his unpleasant personality. He pulled out a key that hung around his neck and unlocked an iron chest beneath the bar. Coins chimed and rustled as Cassius reached in and grabbed coppers and silvers by the fistful.

Emeline slid a full mug of ale across the bar, trailing a river of foam from the head. "Five coppers."

Cassius stood with a scowl. "One silver."

Emeline turned to him and furrowed her brow. The man holding the ale froze with his hand in his purse, a mixed look of confusion and offense.

"Since when?" the man said. "Been paying five coppers an ale for years. And before that it was one!"

Cassius walked over and snatched the mug from the man's hand, splashing ale onto the bar and unfortunate bystanders. "Pay the coin or be gone." He sneered at the man for a moment before turning away and thrusting the mug into Emeline's hands, sloshing ale onto her arms and dress.

Cassius hefted his sack full of coins from the lock box and threw it over his shoulder. The seams strained from the weight. The taproom had gone silent as everyone stopped to watch the spectacle. The only sound came from the jingle of coins and his burdened footsteps as he walked back toward the kitchen door.

Seeming to be suddenly aware of the eyes that were on him, Cassius turned and leered at everyone in the bar. "Fishing trip," he said before turning to walk back into the kitchen.

"Quite the purse for a fishing trip," Emeline said.

Cassius glanced at her, then spat on the bar right in front of Seelios and Garrick before exiting.

"That bastard," Garrick said as he balled his hands into fists.

Seelios stood and put a hand on Garrick's shoulder. "Don't let him trouble you, he's not worth it."

Garrick's eye twitched with anger as he stared at the swinging kitchen door. He slowly sat on his stool and gave Seelios a small nod.

Seelios tapped his chin thoughtfully. "I'm surprised he could lift that. Our boats aren't designed for that sort of weight, be pretty difficult for him to steer."

"And then maybe we'll be rid of him for good," Emeline said as she wiped the thick spit off the bar with a rag. "Here you go, darling. On the house." She dropped the mostly full mug onto the bar in front of Garrick and shook the ale off her arms. She patted her dress with a clean rag and gave a frustrated shake of her head.

The crowd on the other side of the bar became more restless. "Why do those two get all the attention around here? How about you serve some real men, beer wench!"

Emeline whipped her head around and glared at a man in the crowd. "Call me that one more time and I'll chop off your tongue." She jerked a thumb up to the criss-crossing swords on the wall.

Seelios turned to his friend. "Garrick, I really need your help. Please, time is short."

Garrick ignored Seelios's words. He seemed fixated on the crowd that was harassing Emeline. He stood up from his stool, anger building on his face.

"Garrick, please." Seelios reached up and placed another hand on his shoulder. "You're the only one I know who would help me."

"Leave her be," Garrick said to the crowd.

Seelios's hand slid off. It was too late. It was best just to get out of his way.

Two faces turned and gave Garrick an angry stare, but most ignored him. A hand reached out and grabbed Emeline's arm from the other side of the bar. "Why don't you come join us on this side, pretty lass?" Roars of laughter came from the drunken crowd as Emeline struggled to wrestle her arm away.

"I said leave her be!" Garrick stumbled away from his stool and walked over to the crowd.

The laughter stopped, and the men who were slumped onto the bar pushed off their stools and stood. Other patrons at tables went silent and turned to watch. It was shaping up to be quite the entertaining day at the Withertree.

The man who had been the most aggressive with Emeline brought his face up to Garrick's. "Or what, you fool?"

Even from the far end of the bar, Seelios saw Garrick's jaw clench tight with rage. A moment of silence passed between the two men while they glared at each other.

"Just as I thought," the man said as he began to back away. "Just as much a coward as you are worthless."

He spat on Garrick's face and turned back to the bar. "Where's my ale, wench?"

Garrick let out a yell and rushed at the man like a charging bull. They crashed into the row of stools and shattered one of the wooden legs with a crunch. The other men joined the fight, throwing punches and kicks into Garrick's backside while he wrestled on the floor.

Seelios couldn't take the sight of his friend being pummeled. He was tiny compared to even the smallest of the men, but he couldn't stand aside and do nothing. He ran up behind the nearest brawler and threw a punch that landed on the back of his head, sending pain radiating through Seelios's knuckles. The man turned around with a look of annoyance and shoved Seelios to the floor.

"Stay out of this, boy!" The man turned back to the brawl.

Emeline screamed for them to stop, but it had no effect. She turned to the back wall and reached up to grab one of the swords.

The entrance to the tavern swung open with a crash and the brawl slowed as half the men snapped their heads toward the noise. Seelios followed the stupefied gazes of the men and saw his father's large, menacing frame occupying the entrance. He stared at Seelios for a hard moment, then approached the melee. He grabbed the nearest brawler by the collar of his tunic and yanked him backwards. A crowd of onlookers leapt up from their seats as the man crashed into their table, spilling drinks everywhere.

Another man grabbed a chair and swung, breaking it in half across the broad torso of the smith. Seelios's father looked down at the man with quiet fury.

"S—sorry, Ricker, I didn't know it was you!" the drunk man stammered.

The rest of the fighting came to a stop as the other men took note of Ricker's presence. Garrick picked himself up off the floor, blood trickling down his face from a cut on a swollen brow.

"What happened here?" Ricker asked in a tone that would make a lion feel like a kitten.

The men grumbled among themselves.

"They were bothering the lady," Garrick said. He wiped the blood from his face with his sleeve.

"Me and the lads were just having a drink until you got into the middle of it!" one of the men spat.

The others in the group started arguing and shouting over each other at Garrick, building into an inaudible din. Seelios thought another fight was going to break out.

"Enough!" Ricker shouted, silencing the crowd. "Miss Emeline, are you hurt?"

"No, sir, and thank you. Things about got out of hand before you arrived," Emeline said from behind the bar.

"To tell the truth, I had no notion of the brawl. I came for another reason." Ricker shot a stern gaze to Seelios that made him want to shrink into the floor boards.

"What business do you men have getting drunk in the tavern in the middle of the day?" Ricker said to the crowd.

"What of it, Ricker? We do with our time as we please. It doesn't hurt anyone," one of the men said. The others in the group shifted uncomfortably, as if they were unsure they agreed with the statement.

"People in this village break their backs to tend the land yet here you are, drinking the working hours away."

"But, sir, the blight. We can't get but nearly as much the yield," one of the men protested.

"And your solution is to ignore? You're farmers. Your duty is to provide food to the people."

The crowd swayed and shifted uncomfortably. Garrick looked around at the men with a certain satisfaction in his eye.

"Especially you, Garrick. I've heard tales of you drinking in here more than anyone else," Ricker said.

Garrick lowered his head, looking as if he were stung with the same guilt as the rest. The men slowly shuffled out of the tavern without saying a word. One stopped to pick up an overturned stool, but scared away when he saw Ricker watching him.

Garrick followed the last man out, but lingered at Ricker's side. "You're right, Ricker. I should be tending to my—"

"Go home, Garrick. You're too drunk to be working your fields. You'll only end up hurting yourself," Ricker said.

Garrick slunk toward the door, giving a solemn glance to Seelios. "Sorry I didn't help you." He walked out the door.

Emeline cleared her throat and laughed nervously. "You certainly know how to clear a room, Ricker."

"Good day, Miss Emeline." Ricker turned toward the front door and began to walk. He yelled for Seelios to come as he exited the tavern.

Seelios was about to follow his father when something caught his eye on the door frame. He leaned and thought it to be a brown piece of food stuck on the wood, tossed from a table in the mayhem. But something compelled Seelios to investigate further. He reached out and pinched it between his thumb and index finger, causing it to crumble to pieces and fall to the floor, leaving a residue on his hand. Seelios brought it up to his nose then lowered it, giving it a questioning look. It smelled of rich soil pulled from deep within the earth.

3

S eelios walked through the entrance of the forge, expecting to hear the sounds of bellows pumping or hammer striking anvil. Instead, he found a large cloth spread out across the work table, covered with clothes, cookware, camping supplies, and other miscellaneous items. Seelios turned and saw his father rummaging through a chest and pull out a purse that he'd hidden away. Ricker walked over to the table, dropped the purse, wrapped the bundle, and cinched it tight with a rope.

The air in the room was filled with a thick, bitter, and uncomfortable silence.

"I . . . thought your trip to Gorynn wasn't but for another two days," Seelios said.

Ricker continued sifting and packing, refusing to acknowledge Seelios's presence.

"Sorry for not returning sooner," Seelios said with a mumble, watching his father move between shelves and cabinets to pull more items to pack. The silence was almost too much for Seelios. He wanted his father to yell, to tell him how disappointed he was.

Ricker set the bundle aside, laid out another smaller cloth, and began gathering dried meats, fruits, vegetables, and other food.

"I'll need to trade for more fire rock as our current supply was wasted," Ricker said. "I'm leaving early to finish forging my commission at Gorynn Monastery since my current assistance and facilities are insufficient."

The words were said with such calm statement, as if they were a list of facts read off a piece of parchment. They stung more than any amount of yelling could have.

Ricker walked over to another chest and unlocked it with a key. He lifted out a beautiful glass sphere and brought it to the table. The closer Seelios looked, the more he realized it wasn't actually glass. The way it sparkled in the dim light of candles and forge embers, it looked to be something else. Wrapped around it was a single band of swirling metal, the same orichalcum band that his father tempered earlier. Intricate patterns and lines were detailed into the metal, a style that reminded him of the runes that appeared on Seelios's ring. Seelios knew that his father was a master smith, but had no idea that he was capable of crafting such beauty.

Ricker grabbed tools off the wall and brought them to the table. "I'll be gone for several days, possibly weeks." He moved to grab a short sword that leaned against a rack, placed it on the table, and looked at Seelios with a serious stare. "If anyone comes asking for me whom you don't know, you're to hide. If you can't hide, you're to run. If you can't run, you're to defend yourself."

Seelios looked down to the short sword upon the table. It was a speech he heard every time his father traveled.

"Please, can't I just go with you? I can help," Seelios said.

Ricker narrowed his eyes. "You're to stay here and look

after the forge. It's from your negligence that I need to make this journey. You're to scrub this place down until it's spotless. Not a single speck of ash." He fixed Seelios with a fierce, lingering stare, daring him to protest or say something in retort. "Perhaps when I return you'll have learned the discipline to follow through on simple requests."

Seelios felt the heat of anger. "I was going to return with Garrick, but—"

"Enough!" Ricker said, raising his voice.

Seelios's anger was chased away, replaced with a hint of fear.

"One day you must learn that responsibility can't be wished away by juvenile excuses. If you say you're going to do something, you do it. Your delay has cost us much."

Shame took over Seelios. He had so much that he wanted to say, to explain what Garrick was going through. About the cloaked man. Suddenly, he remembered using the runic artifact and his pulse quickened.

Ricker raised an eyebrow at Seelios. "Is there something you want to say?"

Seelios jerked out of his trance and met his father's intimidating gaze. "N—no." Seelios gave a nervous smile that likely raised his father's suspicions even greater. Ricker's piercing silver eyes held for what seemed like an eternity.

"Pack the rest of the fire rock and meet me by the wagon," Ricker said as he gestured toward the small heap of glittering stones in the corner.

Seelios shoveled the rocks into a heavy cloth sack as fast as he could, trying to avoid another scolding. When he finished cinching it tight, he walked it outside the forge and found his father nearly finished preparing the wagon. The weight of the rocks threw Seelios off balance with nearly each step he waddled toward his father.

Ricker's open wagon was hitched to two horses and loaded with the packs that he'd put together inside the forge. Sweat was already beginning to form over Seelios's brow as he wrestled the bag of fire rock toward the rear of the wagon. He tried to lift it up over the edge, but couldn't clear the top of the wheel. He dropped the bag and took a moment to catch his breath. Ricker reached down and grabbed the sack with one hand, lifting it into the wagon with ease. Seelios stepped aside, helpless, as he gave his father room to work.

They loaded the supplies together in continued silence, broken only by Ricker to direct Seelios where to put certain things or where other items could be fetched. Seelios watched as his father tugged and tucked at the wagon load, tying down what needed to be secured. Once the preparations were complete, Ricker climbed into the seat and gathered the reins. Seelios thought his father was going to ride away without any last words, but just as Ricker was about to set the horse into motion he turned and gave Seelios another long stare. It wasn't a look like before; there seemed to be no anger, but a certain sense of concern.

"I feel that, sometimes, I ask too much of you," Ricker said. He raised his eyes up to a black bird flying overhead. "You see that raven? It spends its life soaring from place to place, hunting for its next meal. That is its purpose." He gave a heavy sigh and looked back down. "I know that you seek adventure and, perhaps one day, you will have it. But you must also remember that you are not a raven, your purpose is different. You are but a fawn finding your way in this world, a way that only you can choose. You will find purpose, and when you do it will make you strong."

"Father, please, let me come with you," Seelios said.

Ricker held up a small leather pouch in the air, ignoring the plea. "Mostly silvers and coppers, but I left a few golds. Don't waste it. For food and emergencies only." He placed the pouch in Seelios's hand and the coins inside chimed against each other.

"Another thing," Ricker said. His face turned to a smoldering stare and he pointed down at the ring on Seelios's finger. "Don't disobey my command again." He snapped the reins and the wagon lurched forward.

SEELIOS WAS SWEEPING up a pile of soot when a knock came at the door. A full day had passed since Ricker left, but Seelios could still hear the words inside his head about receiving strangers. He walked over to a window and cracked open one of the shutters. Garrick stood outside, still fresh with healing bruises and cuts across his face. His dirtied outfit from the tavern had been replaced with something much cleaner; a rich green vest over a white linen shirt matched with a fresh pair of linen pants. He was holding the reins to a familiar horse.

Seelios hesitated a moment, then walked to the front door and pulled it open.

"Greetings, friend!" Garrick said with a bright smile. An awkward silence hung in the air for a moment as Seelios stared, unmoving.

Garrick's eyes shifted nervously as he waited for a response. His smile dropped to a solemn expression. "I'm sorry for yesterday. My behavior and not helping you, it was horrendous of me."

Seelios continued to stand in silence, regarding his friend.

Garrick frowned. "I haven't been myself. It's no excuse, but far be it for me to ignore my wrongdoing." He held up the reins to the horse standing next to him. "It may not change yesterday, but she's yours now."

The horse's ears twitched, and she reached out toward Seelios with her nose. Her name was Acorn, a small brown mare that Seelios often visited when he was in Garrick's stables. Acorn barely gave any mind to those who approached her, except for Seelios. It was as if they had a natural connection, an understanding of each other's places in the world.

Seelios had always been fond of animals. In his childhood years he befriended a donkey that let him ride on its back. He'd done it so much that it felt natural to ride horses once he'd grown enough.

Seelios looked back to Garrick. "You're giving her to me?" For a moment, excitement came at the thought of owning Acorn, however, the feeling faded when realization dawned on him. "We don't have room in the stables. Even if we did, I doubt my father would want to keep her."

Garrick shrugged. "I'll keep her in my stables, but she'll be yours. Visit her whenever you like, take her out for rides as you please."

Seelios smiled for the first time since his father left. "I'll trade you," he said as he thrust the broom at Garrick and took Acorn's reins.

Garrick chuckled as he looked at the broom handle. "Suppose I deserved that."

"Hello, girl," Seelios said as he stroked the horse's neck.

Acorn snorted softly and nuzzled Seelios's hand.

Garrick frowned. "I still don't understand her. She's never that affectionate with me."

"It's probably because you call her dim-witted and stupid," Seelios said.

Garrick shook his head and smirked. "That's because she is. Just the other day she got her head stuck in a tree trying to get an apple."

Seelios brushed Acorn's mane with his hand. "She was just hungry."

"There was a pail full of picked apples right next to her."

Seelios shrugged. "Maybe she didn't want the ones you touched."

"The other day she escaped from her stall and ran into the woods."

"Seems to be a smart thing for a captive animal to do."

"She barely made it past the tree line because she got tangled in a bush."

Seelios held up her reins. "Are you going to tie her or should I?"

Garrick waved a hand. "Don't bother. She'll stay if she knows you're here." He walked into the forge with the broom and paused in the doorway, frozen in place.

"Something the matter?" Seelios asked.

Garrick turned and looked over his shoulder at Seelios. "Do you remember that book we found in my library years ago?"

Seelios laughed. "You'll have to be more specific. We found quite a few."

Garrick turned around and faced Seelios with a serious expression. "The one about those demons, the whole manner of them and what they did."

The lingering smile from Seelios's laughter faded. He was the first to find it back then, tucked away on a shadowy shelf. They leafed through it and found chilling sketches of monstrous creatures and myths of war between immortal beings. Seelios always had an interest in learning about the history of the gods, but there was something about that book that made him uneasy. He purposefully pushed the names of the demons as far away from his mind as he could. What he saw in that book he didn't wish upon anyone.

"I . . . vaguely remember," Seelios said. "Why do you ask?"

"It's just, the other day I opened it again. I don't know what compelled me to look, but I found something," Garrick said.

Seelios raised his eyebrows expectedly.

Garrick had a nervous look. "It said that during their height of power the demons could possess the minds of their minions from great distances."

Seelios slowly nodded as he thought about it. The thought was terrifying, but the threat of demons was long eradicated by the gods. They lost the war and were bound for eternity.

"You think that's the cause of your nightmares? Even if they're still alive, I doubt the demons even know we exist. Humans weren't around when demons last roamed free," Seelios said.

Garrick slowly nodded and turned back to the forge. "Aye, you're probably right." He walked in and began sweeping up the soot.

Seelios had never seen his friend so distressed. He walked in, closed the door, and stopped short when he heard the sound of a cork popping from a glass bottle.

"How many is that today?" Seelios said as he furrowed his brow at the flask Garrick had pulled out from his tunic.

"Calm yourself, just little something to lift the spirits. Going to need it if I'm to help you clean this filth." Garrick took a long draw of foamy amber liquid that looked like ale.

"Garrick . . . you shouldn't drink this much."

Garrick threw an annoyed look and corked the bottle. "What are you so concerned about? No harm will come to anyone." He stuffed the flask back into his tunic and began sweeping the floor.

"Except you. It could harm you. I've read—"

"You read what?" Garrick snapped. "You read that taking an occasional sip of ale is bad for you? That I'll be stricken by some plague sent by the gods? Not everything you read is true."

Anger stirred in Seelios's chest. "What's happening with you?" Seelios yelled. If he was a bigger man, he would've tried to punch Garrick, or at least slap some sense into him. "This isn't the friend I know."

"I know!" Garrick yelled back. "I know," he said again in a softer tone, close to a whisper. He turned away from Seelios and leaned on the broom, hanging his head down. He pulled out his flask and took another drink.

"It's the only thing that keeps the nightmares at bay," Garrick said as he wiped his mouth with a sleeve and re-corked the flask.

Garrick turned back to Seelios but averted eye contact. "Without it, I'm haunted by awful things." He looked up at Seelios.

"Garrick, do you remember the day we built the boat?" Seelios asked.

Garrick's distressed face slowly withdrew as he thought about the memory. A small smile crossed over his face. "Gods, that was ages ago. I was about your age now, and you were . . . six years old? We built that shoddy craft in my barn where your father wouldn't see."

Seelios nodded with a smile. "We were so excited to test

it that we took it straight to the river, not even bothering to carry it to the lake. What were we thinking?"

They both chuckled over the thought.

Garrick continued. "Dropped it right into the water, sure it would sink. But it stayed afloat." His smile faded as he recalled what happened after. "Gods, you were so excited. You wanted to see if it could hold you. I was wary of the idea, but you said I could keep the boat from drifting downriver."

Seelios nodded. "I remember."

"I didn't want to. I thought it unsafe, but you begged until I relented. When you jumped in, the jolt of your weight took the boat clear out of my hands. The surge of the river carried you so fast that I couldn't catch you. I watched as you sped away, screaming." Garrick furrowed his brow and looked down. "No matter how fast I ran, the river was faster."

"I was on that boat for the span of nearly four days until you and my father found me. You never gave up looking for me. If it weren't for you, I wouldn't be here. I'd nearly given up on my own life, helpless and afraid, but then the river came to that clearing where you stood. That boat would've been shredded in the rapids if you weren't there to rescue me." Seelios swallowed hard as a lump formed in his throat. "You're like a brother to me, Garrick. And if you keep drinking, I'll lose you."

Garrick drew a heavy breath and looked up as if he were struggling to fight back tears. "I have no choice. I'd rather drink myself into an early grave than endure the pain I'm going through."

A loud knock startled them.

Garrick wiped his eyes, then looked toward the source of the sound. "Are you expecting someone?"

Seelios looked to the door with nerves fluttering in his stomach, then glanced at the short sword that still lay on the work table.

Another knock came. Seelios had almost drawn the weapon when Garrick got up and stood at the window.

Garrick gawked. "There's a wizard at your door!"

Seelios looked at him, confused. Compelled to see for himself, he walked over to the other window. A figure wearing a long white robe stood outside their door with the hood drawn up. Seelios's eyes went wide as he recognized the golden sun emblazoned across the figure's chest. In Garrick's defense, he wasn't that far from the truth. It appeared to be one of the legendary Disciples of Light, a group of humans imbued with the power of Ophanim, God of Light. A disciple had never been to Fembleton, there was never reason to. The man could have been an imposter.

Another knock came, even louder. An old man's muffled voice came from the other side of the door. "I come looking for Ricker Strongheart. I bring news most urgent from Paloise."

"What do we do?" Seelios asked Garrick in a hushed whisper. "My father said any stranger who came looking for him could be dangerous."

Garrick shrugged. "It's just an old man."

"I may be elderly, but I can still hear," the old man said. "Such disrespect. There's no use cowering behind your walls."

Seelios and Garrick stood in silence, trading frantic, silent gestures with each other. Garrick reached for the latch, but Seelios flailed his arms wildly, telling his friend not to open it.

"If you don't come out, I'll let myself in," the old man said. "But, I assure you my way is much messier."

Seelios saw a light build at the bottom of the threshold and shine through the cracks around the frame. An odd sensation of familiarity came over him.

Despite his dad's warning of danger, Seelios ran to the door and yanked it open, revealing the robed man with a ball of glowing light in his hand.

"Most wise. You've saved your door's fate from becoming flaming wreckage," the old man said. He pulled his hand back into his sleeve and the light faded. His eyes shone with silver radiance, just like Ricker. On the road behind him were six armored soldiers mounted on horses, patiently waiting in small formation. A wolf's head was painted onto their towering shields, the sigil of Paloise.

Garrick did a double take, looking from the old man, to Seelios, then back again. He had a look of wordless confusion, just as Seelios did. Up until that moment, Seelios thought he and his father were the only ones with eyes of silver.

"Take me to Ricker, immediately. I must speak with him at once," the old man said.

"Ricker isn't here," Seelios said. He took a large swallow, nervous about giving too much information.

"I see." The old man narrowed his eyes, then widened them. "Forgive me. In my haste, I've forgotten my manners. I'm Gregory, herald of Ophanim and Disciple of Light." He extended his hand.

Seelios grabbed Gregory's hand and shook. "Seelios, smith's apprentice."

Gregory looked down and frowned. "Come now, boy. A proper handshake has a firm grip behind it."

Seelios tried to squeeze harder but doubted it was strong enough to satisfy. "This is my friend, Garrick."

"A pleasure," Gregory said as he took Garrick's hand,

looking at him with a smile that slowly dropped away. Something that almost looked like intense concern glimmered in the disciple's eye.

Garrick dropped his hand and disappeared back into the forge, leaving them in silence. Gregory stroked his beard, deep in thought as he watched Garrick's retreating back. "Interesting. Well, I'll be off then. I suppose I'll find Ricker on the road to Gorynn."

Seelios was taken aback. He didn't mention anything about where his father had gone. He tried to think if it was possible for disciples to read minds, but didn't recall anything of the sort. Then again, the power of the gods wasn't something to be trifled with.

"Is there something you'd like me to pass on to the smith when he returns?" Seelios called after Gregory as he walked to his pack-laden horse by the group of soldiers.

The disciple paused for a moment, then turned. "This is a message I best deliver myself; however, if by chance I don't find him on the road, tell him that the gate has been destroyed."

Seelios felt confused. "Is this a gate in Paloise?"

Gregory climbed onto his horse. "He'll know."

4
_____

Seelios and Garrick continued the day cleaning the forge, exchanging few words. They swept and re-swept the entire floor of the workshop, followed by heavy scrubbing until there was nothing left but the bare stone foundation. The only visible spots were scorch marks of accidents years passed, most from Seelios.

Fiddling with the stone ring on his finger, he wondered how his father knew he'd used it in the tavern. If he saw from the window, surely he would've stepped into the tavern sooner. Still, if Ricker was away, it would be impossible to know if Seelios used it again.

Seelios turned to Garrick and broke the many hours of silence. "If you really think this ring will help you, we can try again."

Garrick pulled his head out of the furnace, soot all over his face. He thought for a moment and waved a hand at Seelios. "Wouldn't change anything." He reached back into the furnace with a brush. "I already know what it would reveal."

Seelios looked down at the ring. Garrick might have been sure, but Seelios wasn't.

The runes had nearly appeared again when shouts came from outside. Seelios and Garrick exchanged curious glances and raced around the work table to reach a window. Fembleton's middle-aged tailor was running toward the forge, calling out in a flurry of panic.

"Mr. Wallman, what is it?" Seelios said as he ran outside.

The tailor pointed frantically. "My boat; seize it before its lost!"

Seelios turned to the lake and saw an unmanned fishing boat floating downriver. Throughout his childhood he often played by the water, occasionally catching the errant rope or fishing spear dropped by someone in the lake, but an entire boat was unheard of. He looked upriver and, for the first time in his life, saw the rusty bars of the bridge gate raised.

"I've got it," Seelios said as he ran into the forge. He grabbed a large push broom caked with ash.

Garrick followed. "You can't possibly think to grab that boat with that."

Seelios looked out the window and saw it was drawing near. "Tell your future sons and daughters of this tale of courage." He ran past Garrick with a smile.

"Seelios, don't be a fool." Garrick spun and chased after him.

The current of the river was surprisingly strong when Seelios stepped into the bank. Cold water lapped up around his calves and drenched the cuffs of his pants. He held the push broom out like a spear as he watched the boat like a cat ready to pounce.

Garrick splashed into the water. "You'll drown yourself, don't—"

The push broom hooked the inside of the boat with a

thunk and scraped along the gunwale. The thought of saving Mr. Wallman's boat was exhilarating, Seelios had never been a hero before. The enthrallment, however, distracted him just enough to forget to brace himself in the soft silt of the river. The broom caught the pointed aft and pulled so hard that he lost a boot. He became airborne for a moment, then crashed into the water face first, fast in tow while holding onto the broom handle.

Intermittent yells came from the shore as Seelios struggled to keep his head above water. His muscles tensed from the shocking cold and his hands began to slip. Something grabbed him around the ankle and pulled, tossing him back into the shallows of the river. He picked himself up and stood on legs shaking in the rushing current. Garrick was wrestling the boat to shore just a little further down river.

"Gods be good, boy." The tailor said, chest heaving from his sprint. "Get out of the water, will you? Before you get yourself killed." He held out a hand.

Seelios took hold of the tailor and pulled himself onto the muddy bank.

"A brave thing you did back there, but damn foolish. Damn foolish indeed. What would your father have said?" the tailor asked.

Seelios wrung his clothes and watched Garrick drag the boat ashore. "I just thought I could save it."

"Be a bit of time before I can get this up to the docks," Garrick called out.

"Don't trouble yourself. You lads have done enough," Mr. Wallman said. "That damned innkeep must've left the bridge gate open. He'll rue the day he thought he could steal my boat and get away with it."

Garrick scoffed as he walked up to them. "That gate's been rusted shut for ages, one man couldn't have lifted that thing. That withering old bastard barely has enough meat on his bones to carry his own weight."

Seelios looked to the bridge again, rusty tines raised like a claw from the lake.

"Seelios, I must ask one more thing of you. May I leave this boat here? It will only be until tomorrow once I've fetched the men to return it to the lake."

Seelios nodded. "Of course, but we could—"

"No, lad. This is a cause of my carelessness, letting Cassius borrow my boat. I thought he was just using it to fish the lake, not escape town."

SEELIOS AND GARRICK said their goodbyes to the tailor and walked back into the forge to finish their work. It wasn't long after they resumed their chores that the shaking came. At first, Seelios thought Garrick was moving the anvil across the floor, but the ground became so violent that it felt as if the Southern Mountains were crumbling to pieces.

Seelios could barely stay on his feet as he stumbled out the front door and onto the dirt road. The shriveled stalks of wheat were swaying to something more than just the blowing breeze. Trees danced to unheard music. Acorn lifted her head from a patch of grass and looked toward the lake.

Garrick stumbled out. "What in gods is happening?"

Seelios saw villagers rushing out of shops and homes near the village square, looking around with confusion. Shouts came as the vibrating earth grew in ferocity, and a humming filled the air.

The water of the lake swelled up over the tops of the buildings, sending a rippling wave that crawled towards town, growing larger as it approached. Before anyone had any time to react, the wave crested like an ominous blue wall, casting a great shadow over Fembleton, and crashed into stone and wood, ripping through homes and shops. Water gushed between the buildings and over the cobblestone of the square.

Seelios and Garrick instinctively backed away as the wave splashed toward them, but by the time it reached the forge it had lost much of its strength. Acorn whinnied and pawed her hoofs in the air as water rushed over the ground like a shallow flood. The force of the retreating water caught Seelios off guard, and he stumbled to the ground with a splash. Garrick rushed over and helped him up. Seelios's clothes sagged off his limbs for a second time that day as he tried to wring them dry. The mud and dirt would take many washes to get out, if they came out at all.

A towering column of jagged stone stood in the lake, resembling an enormous fist that had punched out of the earth. It stood so tall that it cast a shadow that nearly spanned all the way to the shore. Sounds of grinding rock echoed over the water as stone fingers slowly opened and flexed in the air, cascading water down the length of the arm. Trees and bushes sprouted between the jointed plates of rock that covered the stony limb, as if it had once been a part of the very mountains themselves.

The turbulent waters of the lake swelled again as a face rose out of the water, like a giant man waking from his slumber deep underground. Its forehead and cheeks were smooth as worn granite except where cracks appeared in place of wrinkles. Thick green moss hung down from its head and chin in place of hair. Its eyes were brilliant diamonds that sparkled in the sun.

The stone figure rose out of the water, revealing an enormous torso of sharp rock and shimmering minerals. Water broke over its shoulders like the falls of a mountain spring. It stood upright and cast its diamond gaze toward the village.

"Gods help us all," Garrick whispered behind Seelios.

Seelios watched the stone giant with fascination glistening in his eyes. "I think that *is* one of the gods. If my gut were true, the God of Earth."

Garrick turned to Seelios with a look of disbelief. "How do you find yourself excited at a time like this? That foul thing just razed half the village!"

Flocks of birds rose out of the surrounding woods and flew to the crown of the god's head, circling it like the peak of a majestic mountain. Deer, rabbits, foxes, and other woodland animals came running out from Fembleton's forests and skittered toward the edge of the lake to gaze up at the earthly figure. Even Acorn sprinted to join the other animals, followed by other horses that broke out of their stables, some pulling carts and wagons from the market square.

If Seelios had any doubts of which god it was before, he was sure of it now. The God of Earth commanded all forest animals and creatures to his will, except for those that are in devoted service to other gods. Even domesticated horses bent to the god's presence.

The ground shuddered beneath them as the towering stone god strode toward the town, sending waves that lapped up against the broken debris of wrecked homes. Villagers in the square screamed, running around in the chaos of shaking earth and flooding water as the colossal giant approached. Many ran to the stables only to find their horses gone and resorted to fleeing on foot.

"Seelios, we need to leave," Garrick urged as he watched the god slowly make his way across the lake.

Seelios's excitement grew as he continued to watch the massive figure. "What is a god doing in Fembleton?" Seelios said, ignoring Garrick.

Garrick regarded Seelios with an annoyed look. "What does it matter? We're in danger."

Seelios looked at the destruction of the market square, pools of water trembling on the cobblestone. Some people lay injured on the ground, some struggling to swim back to shore after being pulled into the lake from the wave's retreat. It was unlike a god to destroy so carelessly.

"But still . . . there's something happening here. I wish to know what," Seelios said.

The baker's shop crunched under an enormous foot in an explosion of rock and timber as the god stepped out from the lake, bringing half of the neighboring shop to ruins with it. The towering figure looked down at the people scurrying away from him. Woodland animals scampered around the god's feet in a wide circle, splashing in the puddles of water like a litter of excited puppies.

The granite lips of the face cracked open to reveal a dark chasm inside. "Ricker," the god said with a deep, booming voice. Seelios's heart skipped at the sound of his father's name.

The stone figure's diamond gaze swept back and forth over the town, searching. "If you don't reveal yourself, I'll destroy this entire village."

Another foot came down and crushed a house beside the lake. People ran, screaming, while one tried to crawl away without any use of his legs.

"Don't think that you can hide from your responsibilities forever," the God of Earth boomed. "I know you're here. Your presence is no longer a secret. I can feel you."

Seelios's eyes widened. His mind went to the ring his

father gave him. Such a powerful relic couldn't have been in his possession by chance. Somehow, Ricker was connected to the gods.

Out of the corner of his eye, Seelios noticed someone standing in the shriveled wheat field. He recognized the figure as the cloaked man from the tavern, the same who saw him use the ring. Seelios called out to him, but he fled toward the lake in his stiff-legged gait. The hood of the man's cloak flew back and revealed a head that was missing the entire right side of the skull, as if he were born without it. It suddenly made sense why he chose to hide part of his face in the tavern.

The God of Earth looked down as the half-faced man arrived at the base of his foot and turned to point a finger at Seelios. The god's diamond eyes narrowed into slits and searched until they locked onto Seelios.

Seelios's curiosity quickly turned to fear, and he began to back away. "Garrick, he's looking—."

The towering god's stone skin began to shimmer and gleam like the surface of a sparkling ore. Large cracks spread across his chest, traveling down his arms and legs, and let out an eerie green light. The sound of the rock ripping apart was thunderous and deafening.

The ring of birds around the god's head scattered as they flew fast and far away. The woodland animals scrambled in a similar chaotic motion, sprinting and hopping away to the nearest tree line. Men tried to jump onto horses as they raced through the ruined town, but none succeeded in capturing a steed. Seelios caught a flash of Acorn's fur before she disappeared into the woods by the tavern.

The god lifted its head, raising both arms as its colossal form exploded, launching massive chunks of rock and debris in all directions. Seelios covered his ears, but it did little to drown out the cacophony. Boulders rained down like meteors, smashing village shops and homes like they were made of twigs and paper. Among impacts of falling stone, Seelios heard the screams of the villagers.

A large boulder nearly struck the forge and landed mere steps away from where Seelios stood. The shock made his knees buckle, and he tumbled to the ground as clumps of dirt and grass showered down. The boulder slid, gouging the earth before it rolled into the wheat field.

A small mountain of rubble stood next to the lake shore where the stone god once stood. When the dust settled, a man in brilliant shining armor was standing at its peak, wielding a large axe adorned with glowing runes along its surface resembling those of Seelios's ring. The metal of the axe gleamed and swirled with orichalcum luster.

The armored man's face resembled the colossal stone form except, instead of a beard of green moss, his hair was dark as midnight. The man's powerful looking eyes flashed with green light. He turned to the half-face man who stood patiently among the rubble, still pointing at Seelios. The armored man turned his gaze and met Seelios's eyes.

The God of Earth raised his axe into the air, and its runes blazed with intensity. Bright lines of green light spread out across the surfaces of the boulders scattered through the village. They raced and circled, inscribing more runes like a dozen invisible hands. The boulder in the wheat field stirred and rocked as arms and legs unfolded. It stood, a smaller version of the colossal stone god from earlier, and reared a small and lumpy head toward Seelios, staring with haunting green eyes of light.

Seelios watched in awe as the animated boulder stomped out of the field. He felt the tug of Garrick's hand.

"Stop your gawking!" Garrick yelled.

They turned and ran down river toward the forest. They took but ten steps when the earth exploded before them, raising a curtain of blinding dust and raining down dirt from overhead. Seelios raised his hands as he was pelted with pebbles and clumps of mud. When the dust cleared he saw a wide wall of jagged stone that stretched to either side, blocking their retreat. The river crashed into the stone wall and began to swell over its banks.

"Gods be damned," Garrick said.

The God of Earth's stone creature came thundering behind them and snatched up Seelios with such ferocity that it forced the air from his lungs. Its grip was so tight that Seelios thought his ribs might snap like dry twigs.

Garrick kicked the creature in the leg, but it seemed to have no effect. He winced in pain as he limped backward. The creature looked down and pulled its arm back, raising its free hand. Garrick tried to scramble out of range, but the arm came down in a blur and giant stone finger tips made contact with his face. He spun through the air like a pinwheel before landing on the ground and tumbling into the wheat field.

Seelios tried to call out to his friend, but his lungs were squeezed so tight he couldn't even get out a whisper. The stone creature stomped toward the God of Earth, brandishing its prize in the air. Seelios looked back and saw Garrick lying on the ground, unmoving. In the distance the rock wall crumbled, sending up sprays of water as it fell back into the river. The water surged over the fallen barricade and continued down its age old path.

Throughout the village, similar stone creatures with glowing runes climbed out of the craters and ruined houses. They varied in size, but some were so massive they towered over standing shops.

Seelios hit the ground in a painful drop, coughing and gasping for air in front of the God of Earth.

"This is the one you saw?" the god asked the half-face man.

He nodded with one expressionless eye fixed on Seelios.

"Your work here is done." The god reached out and touched the man on the cheek with a finger. Cracks spread over his face and down his neck like mud baking under the sun. The cloak dropped as he crumbled to the ground in a pile of dried up clay.

"Your ring," the God of Earth said. "Where did you get it?"

Before Seelios could reply, a blinding flash came from the market square.

The God of Earth turned and his face met with a beam of light that exploded on impact, radiating an intense heat and turning Seelios's vision white and spotty. The sound of several galloping horses came, and a strong hand grabbed Seelios, hoisting him up onto a saddle.

"F—father?" Seelios asked, vision still blurry from the flash.

"Afraid not, boy," a familiar man said.

"We'll keep the god distracted," another voice said. "Escape with him while you still can."

"Be wary of his axe. Nothing can withstand its edge," the familiar man said.

The horse skid to a sudden stop, lurching Seelios forward, nearly out of the saddle.

"Whoa, there! Onward, you confounded—"

The horse started bucking wildly, whinnying at ear-piercing volumes. Seelios tried to hold onto the saddle with what little strength his grip could muster, but it didn't take long before Seelios was tossed high into the air. He landed hard on the ground to the sound of something like a thick tree snapping in half. Excruciating pain radiated up his leg and throughout his whole body.

Shouts of surprise came from men in armored plate falling to the ground with a metallic rattle.

"Curses, how could I forget? Get up, boy!" the familiar man said.

"My leg," Seelios said through gritted teeth. "I think it's broken."

His right leg ached with a feeling so intense that it made him nauseous.

"That boat will have to do then."

Two arms scooped Seelios up, causing him to cry out when his leg dangled in the air. Even the pull of gravity on his shattered bone was enough to send electric jolts of agony through his body. The dizzying pain, combined with his blurred vision, made it hard for him to orient himself, feeling as if the world was spinning around him. The last thing he heard before his vision tunneled to black was the booming voice of an angry god.

5

Garrick's head ached liked it had been caught between a hammer and an anvil. He slowly cracked open his eyes and saw dancing stars, zipping around like fireflies. Blue sky showed through a forest of brown and black wheat, bobbing and swaying sadly in the breeze. Even among the dancing lights he could see the Daylight Star twinkling above, brighter than usual. For reasons he could not explain, the sight of it haunted him to his core.

He expected to hear the whistle of the wind as it blew through the crops, but instead found his hearing muted by a high pitched ringing. Garrick pulled himself upright and his stomach lurched. He turned and vomited, the bitter smell of regurgitated ale rose from the ground to meet his nose, inducing another heave from his stomach that yielded nothing but dribbles of liquid and wheezing. He wiped thick spit that clung to his lip and looked around at his surroundings. He couldn't remember how he got there, or even what he had done earlier that day. Memories kept fading in and out as he struggled to recall something as simple as his last meal.

He slowly climbed to his feet. Overwhelming dizziness nearly caused him to fall back down, but he managed to take a few steps with the grace of a newborn fawn. He brushed through the plagued wheat and found himself standing before Fembleton's forge. An odd line of stone rubble curved from behind the building and passed through the field. Feelings of familiarity entered Garrick's mind when he saw the scars in the earth, but he still couldn't recall what happened.

His eyes fell back on the forge and noticed its front door was ripped off and cast aside. Splinters of wood frayed out from the hinges.

"Seelios!" Garrick shouted. He couldn't tell how far his voice carried with the persisting ring in his ears.

Garrick fumbled his hands over his body to see if he was wearing a weapon, but found nothing on his belt. He was ill-equipped to fight any bandits, but he'd be damned if he stood by when his friend was in need.

The inside was as much of a mess as the door. Furniture was turned over and broken in several places. Tools were scattered about, bags of sand and coal were poured out across the floor. The place was an utter disaster. Garrick wondered if Seelios and Ricker had made a mess of things trying to gather supplies, but there would've been no need to go out of their way to destroy their property. He looked at the anvil that had even been tipped onto its side, cracks in the stone floor reached out from the impact of its enormous weight. The amount of strength it would've taken to move that thing was far beyond his frail friend, but perhaps not Ricker. Even still, Ricker had a deliberate way of doing things. No matter the circumstance or state of emergency,

Ricker always seemed to act with careful planning. The chaos of the forge didn't seem like anything Ricker would've done. What happened must've been at the hands of someone else. The thought chilled Garrick's spine. He couldn't even think of the last time there was a threat of bandits in their part of the continent. Especially a town that was supposedly under the protection of a god. Perhaps the blight was making people truly desperate.

Garrick felt a subtle shake of the earth beneath his feet. He stepped over a broken chair and walked to the window. In the distance he saw a farmer running down the cobbled road out of the market square. The look on his face was one of sheer terror, throwing glances over his shoulder as if he were fleeing something in hopeless desperation.

Shuddering vibrations in the ground followed in quick succession as a large stone figure covered with glowing glyphs stomped after him. It caught up to the man in five strides and lifted him into the air. The man squirmed in the stone beast's grip for a moment before the thing slammed him into the ground, sending a spray of blood that colored the road and stained the surrounding grass. Garrick backed away from the window, horrified. The image of the same creature came surging back into his head, holding Seelios hostage in the air.

Panic beginning to mount within his chest, Garrick ran out of the forge and looked for some sign of his friend. There was nothing but the crumbling ruins of Fembleton as it was torn to pieces by behemoths made of earth. Stone creatures with lines of light and glowing runes were ambling around the wreckage, tossing things out of the way and sifting through remains. He remembered the God of Earth appearing in the lake and raining down destruction, searching for Seelios's father. With Ricker gone the god must've left to continue his search, leaving his minions to terrorize in his wake.

Garrick tried to calm himself and think. The circumstances that led up to his waking in the wheat field were beginning to dawn on him. His face felt tender and hot. He reached up to touch it and winced. When he pulled his hand away his fingers were wet with blood. The stone creature must've struck him quite a blow. The fact that he was still in one piece was a miracle.

He looked again at the creatures walking through the town, making an utter mess of things. He didn't know the fate of Seelios, but others might still need help. His thoughts drifted to Emeline.

Garrick turned to the forest. If he fled into the thick of the trees he might be able to escape the stone creatures, but he couldn't shake the thought of Emeline being in danger. He ran back into the forge and sifted through debris. The disarray of the place made it unrecognizable, but he'd remembered where most things were. He righted a fallen weapons rack and a long sword clattered to the ground. He sheathed it and tied it to his belt.

On his way to the square Garrick almost lost a boot to the thick mud of the water-logged dirt road. When he reached the cobbled stone he got a closer look at the destruction. Half of the buildings were missing most of their walls, as if they were cracked open like eggs and stripped of their insides. An overturned wagon bobbed in the water among large pieces of splintered wood that had once made up the foundation of a house.

Garrick barely made it past two shops when he felt vibrations in the ground. He scrambled for cover and crouched behind the remains of the tailor shop. He peered around the crumbling wall and saw one of the stone giants across the cobbled road, glowing green eyes slowly sweeping the area. They must have been constructs serving the God of Earth, but he couldn't think of a single reason why a god would want to destroy their town.

The creature's gaze drifted toward Garrick, forcing him to duck further behind the wall. He held his breath and prayed that he wasn't seen. His last attempt to attack one of those things didn't end well, so his only option was to hide like a scared mouse. Shaking footsteps got closer until they felt like they were nearly upon him. Small pebbles and dust fell down his neck as he pressed his body against the wall, trying to stay out of sight.

Garrick noticed movement to his right and saw the tailor's wife trying to crawl from under a pile of debris. She grabbed at the ground with her hands, but couldn't pull herself free. She turned and looked at Garrick, desperation in her eyes. She reached out to him, mouth pleading with what Garrick could only imagine were cries for help. Heavy steps vibrated like an earthquake and a shadow blanketed the area as the stone giant scooped her up. Garrick watched in horror as the colossal thing crushed her in one hand like a toy doll. Despite his loss of hearing, he could still imagine her screams as he watched her face of torment in the moments before her death.

Garrick got up and ran while the giant was occupied, wondering what he had gotten himself into, why he hadn't just fled into the forest while he had the chance. At least twice he rushed inside a half-standing house as a stone creature walked past. He noticed that the glowing patterns on their skin looked just like the glyphs that appeared on Seelios's ring. He huddled next to the corner edge of the cobbler shop and saw the Withertree Tavern and Inn standing at the edge of town. He breathed a heavy sigh of relief upon seeing the building, still standing whole. Its windows were boarded up from the inside, a sign people barricaded themselves within.

Garrick ran with reckless abandon, desperate to see if Emeline was there. He slid along the side wall of the tavern facing the forest and gave a knock on the window. One of the boards pulled away and a man appeared. He and Garrick made eye contact, and the man turned from the window and yelled something. Emeline's pretty face appeared in a flash of red hair, her eyes wide with amazement. Garrick's heart fluttered at the sight of her.

Emeline mouthed something excitedly as she pointed to the tavern entrance. Garrick tried to communicate back to her, wanting to tell her that it wasn't safe to stay in the tavern, but she disappeared before he could finish. He peered around the corner and looked at the ruined remains of the market square. The heads of the rock creatures bobbed up and down as they stomped between buildings.

The door swung open, and Emeline poked her head out. She gestured at Garrick to come inside, saying something that he couldn't hear. Just as he was halfway to the door, a rock giant stepped out from behind the cobbler's shop and held its gaze in their direction.

Emeline didn't seem to notice the approaching monster until the thundering footsteps shook the earth beneath their feet. She turned, eyes wide with horror, seeing the thing nearly upon them. She pulled Garrick into the tavern and slammed the door, bolting it shut as if that were to deter anything from following them inside. She slowly backed away from the quake of the approaching monster, wearing a look of deep concern. The tavern was filled with men, women, and children all wearing looks of tear-filled terror.

Emeline turned to Garrick and said something, panic

written across her face. Garrick gestured toward his ear and said at an inappropriately loud volume, "My hearing; I can barely understand what you're saying." He glanced toward the door. "We can't stay here."

A plank of wood struck Garrick in the shoulder as the door caved inward, wrought iron twisted out of place and boards broke clean in half. The building shook as a massive hand of rock ripped through the inn on the second floor and pulled down a cascade of rafter beams, stone, and plaster.

Chaos ensued as people tried to run from falling rubble. Garrick drew his sword and swung at the stone arm that grasped around the tap room, but sparks flew as the blade glanced off harmlessly. He struggled to hold onto the weapon vibrating in his hands, his arms stinging from the attempt.

Emeline pulled at Garrick's shoulder and shouted something that he couldn't hear. He sheathed his sword and pointed in the direction of the bar.

"Back door," Garrick yelled.

Emeline turned to look and nodded.

They wove through the obstacles of tables and escaped out the door that led to the kitchen. They raced past sacks full of food and lines of hanging cookware that swayed in the air. The entire building shook, threatening to fall to pieces as the stone monster tore through the building.

They escaped out the back of the tavern just in time to see half of the building collapse in on itself. Garrick thought about all the people inside. The rock giant was still picking through the rubble and tossing away whole pieces of the structure.

Not daring to brave the open Trade Road, they ran toward the thick forest that spanned behind the Withertree, hoping not to be followed. Garrick felt the yank of Emeline's hand on his own, making him realize that they'd been joined almost the entire time. The revelation made him blush and forget about the dangers of the present, just for a moment.

Emeline pointed at something struggling against some branches in a tree.

Garrick reached for his sword and took a closer look. He couldn't believe his eyes when he recognized the familiar shape.

"Acorn!" Garrick shouted. His face lit up as he ran over to the terrified horse. "I've never been happier to see you."

Acorn's eyes were wild with fear and she jerked her head away from Garrick's touch. The horse struggled against her tangled reins against branches and leaves, shaking them wildly.

Garrick backed away, trying not to provoke her further. If those branches broke, she would bolt.

Acorn's demeanor seemed to soften as Emeline approached. She stroked the animal's neck and whispered with such tenderness that, despite being unable to hear, even made Garrick feel calmer. She reached up and slowly undid the tangled reins while she continued to soothe.

"Well done," Garrick said with an impressed look. He lifted Emeline onto the saddle and hopped on behind her, kicking the horse into a full gallop.

6

Seelios sat upright in a flurry of motion that sent waves of pain through his whole body. He shut his eyes and let himself fall to his back, grimacing as he felt the throb of every bruise on his ribs and the fiery pain of his leg. The gentle sounds of water were all around him as he bobbed up and down.

"You should be still, boy. You can't heal if you're thrashing about," a voice said behind him.

Seelios craned his neck and saw Gregory, the Disciple of Light. Seelios's muscles were unable to hold the awkward position and he let his body flop back down onto the hard wood, sending the boat into a gentle rock.

The Daylight Star twinkled above as he stared into the sky. Since Garrick had mentioned it, it did appear a bit unusual.

"Where are we?" Seelios asked.

"The Brascella River, west of Fembleton. You've been unconscious for nearly two hours," the disciple said.

Seelios looked around and recognized the boat he'd tried to save for Mr. Wallman earlier that day.

"That light earlier . . . you saved me?" Seelios asked.

"I did," Gregory said.

"Did anyone else survive?"

Silence filled the air. Seelios's thoughts drifted to Garrick lying in the wheat field.

"My friend, did he make it?"

"I don't know the fate of your friend, but I fear once the god unleashed his golems there was little chance of survival."

Seelios went quiet. The lapping of the water against the boat was soothing, yet the anxiety of what had happened moments before was just beginning to set in. Seelios's breath grew heavy as he thought about all of those people getting crushed and stomped by the stone monstrosities. Gods weren't supposed to do such terrible things.

Tears began to fill Seelios's eyes as emotions swelled inside him.

"Why would a god do something like that?" Seelios asked, trying his best not to scream. "We didn't do anything. Those people didn't deserve to die like that!"

"You must calm down. We can't let ourselves be discovered," Gregory said. He turned his head to look behind him, then slowly scanned the surrounding trees.

"I know not what provoked Gameus to attack your village. It's unlike him, or any god, to massacre mortals," Gregory said.

Seelios had never heard that name before, but had seen it written down plenty of times in the books chronicling the gods. Gameus was the true name of the God of Earth. He realized that he'd been pronouncing it wrong this entire time.

"What did he want with you?" Gregory asked.

Seelios hesitated for a moment, wondering how much

he should reveal. He figured since Gregory was a Disciple of Light that he must be trustworthy. He did save his life after all.

Seelios lifted his hand up. "He asked me about my ring. It's . . . a bit unique."

"That it is. A very precious piece of jewelry you have there," Gregory said.

Seelios craned his neck to look at the disciple, who smiled back at him.

"How do you know?" Seelios asked.

"I know quite a bit about that ring, there are several like it," Gregory said. "But tell me, what else did the God of Earth say?

"That was all," Seelios said. He thought for a moment and then widened his eyes with realization. "He was also looking for my father, just as you were. What has everyone got to do with him? Is this about the gate?"

Gregory let a short moment of silence pass before he answered. "Yes, and things may be worse than I thought," Gregory said.

"Did you find my father? Is he safe?" Seelios asked.

"I'm afraid I didn't, which only complicates matters," Gregory said. "The news I meant to deliver will have to wait," Gregory said in a lowered whisper, as if he were trying to hide even the notion that he kept the information that he did. "He'd already made his way deep into the Southern Mountains. When I felt the God of Earth drawing near, we had to return to Fembleton. We'll contact your father once we've reached Paloise. I'm sure he'll be eager to know you're safe."

"Why did you risk your life to come back? Those soldiers, they gave their lives for us to escape."

"It's my sworn duty. In Ophanim's absence it's the job of

the disciples to protect those within his realm. Just as it is the duty of the other gods to protect those within their realms."

"Yet the God of Earth attacked us."

Silence came as the water lapped against Gregory's oar. If the God of Earth was attacking people, there was a possibility that other gods may be doing the same. Seelios thought of his father being attacked in the mountains by the Goddess of Wind. He tried his best to push the thought out of his head.

"We need to find somewhere to rest," Gregory said. "We've no provisions, and you're in no shape to make the journey all the way to Paloise. However, I'm afraid I don't know the lands as well by river as I do by road."

Seelios slowly lifted himself onto one shaking arm and scanned for familiar landmarks. Although he rarely traveled far beyond the foothills of Fembleton, he had a strong knowledge of the geography of the continent of Inf. The countless hours Seelios spent in Garrick's library led him to stumble on a great many of useful tomes, some of which were detailed atlases.

Seelios thought for a moment as he considered the towns closest to Fembleton, particularly those near the river. There was a town called Alnerwick nestled deeper into the woods that would take some effort to reach, but still a better option than trying to float downriver for days without food.

"If we stop at the first bend there's another village to the northeast. We'd have to trek on foot for some time." Seelios thought about his leg and realized how difficult it would prove. He wasn't even sure he could manage.

"We passed that bend some time ago, perhaps a quarter or half-hour before you woke," Gregory said.

Seelios's heart sank. The river must have been running faster than usual.

"Are there no more towns?" Gregory asked. "The closest one I know is Pinewood. The God of Water has a life-giving monolith there, perhaps we could use it to summon his aid. Still, it's doubtful you'd survive that long. We need something closer. "

Pinewood the Forest Water Village was a place that Seelios had always wanted to see some day, but Gregory was right; it was quite far. There was no other alternative.

Seelios shook his head. "No other village is near unless we go back."

The water whooshed at the forceful push of Gregory's paddle. He dug into the river with surprising strength, turning the boat toward the bank.

Trudging out from the water was the first time Seelios saw Gregory with his hood down. Beneath the white hair, he noticed a network of thick scars that ran along his neck. Similar scars appeared on his arms when the sleeves of his robes were pushed back to pull the boat ashore. Seelios blushed when Gregory caught him staring. "Sorry, I didn't mean to—"

"Worry not, boy, I wear these scars proudly. They remind me of a sacrifice I made for Ophanim. One that all the disciples had to make, and did so without hesitation," he said.

They pulled the boat through the river shallows and up into the tree line. After they'd covered it in leaves and branches, Seelios pointed out the general direction of Alnerwick.

The amount of time it took to move through the forest was vastly overestimated. Seelios's leg was splinted and padded with thick cloth, making it difficult for him to move. In the little ground they were able to cover, Seelios needed frequent breaks for rest. He found himself lacking in strength even more than his normal self.

"Here," Gregory said as he reached inside his robes. He pulled out a smooth river stone.

"What is it?" Seelios asked between gulps of water from a skin.

"Something that can ease the pain. And possibly more." Gregory placed the stone in Seelios's palm

Seelios regarded it, turning it over a few times in his hand. He looked up at Gregory expectantly.

"Am I supposed to do something with it?" Seelios asked.

Gregory looked down at Seelios with an arched eyebrow. "You feel nothing?"

Seelios shook his head.

Gregory held an expression of slight disappointment. "What you hold in your hand is a runic artifact of certain healing properties, called a rejuvenation stone. This particular artifact has been innate for some time, much like your ring was until you came into possession of it."

Seelios suspected that the ring his father had given him was a runic artifact, but with all the secrecy that surrounded it, he never dared bring up the subject. Now he was holding another in his palm. It was a dream come true for someone who was hardly allowed outside of the limits of their small hometown.

Seelios looked at the artifact with wonder. He closed his eyes and tried to focus on it in the same manner he'd done with his ring, but felt nothing. He saw the stone in his mind, but it was nothing but an empty shell, like trying to draw a bucket of water from a well long dried up.

Seelios opened his eyes and frowned.

"Here," Seelios said as he lifted it back up to Gregory. "It doesn't seem to be working."

Gregory held up a hand. "I suspect you just need time with it. I'm curious, how long was it before you could use that ring of yours?" He gestured toward the stone band on Seelios's finger.

Seelios looked down at his hand. "I had it for the span of a few days, maybe a week, before the runes appeared."

Gregory stroked his short beard thoughtfully. "I see. Fascinating."

"What?" Seelios asked.

"It's just, you've managed to accomplish something that would require the combined focus of many disciples at once. That ring lost its runic luster many a year ago, rendered inert through over use. Yet, somehow you've managed to reawaken it without assistance." He raised an eyebrow. "You didn't have assistance, correct?"

Seelios shook his head. "I was alone." He looked down at his ring again. He hadn't realized it was such an accomplishment to activate it. He'd wondered if his father knew what he had done, if maybe that was why his use of the artifact had to be kept such a secret.

Gregory pulled out another object from his robes and held it up. It looked like a miniature stone tower with a glass marble cradled at the top. It reminded Seelios of a piece that belonged to a game set of some kind, the type a child lordling might play with.

"Tell me, Seelios. What do you know of the abilities of the God of Light?"

Seelios thought for a moment, turning his gaze up and to the side as he thought back to what he read in books and heard from stories. "He wields a burning light to smite his opponents. His eyes could see the hidden truth. His touch could heal even the most grievous of wounds." He drifted off into silence as he struggled to remember more.

The traits of the gods were native to their natural element. Books were inconsistent on many accounts of what specific powers the gods possessed, but nearly all of them agreed that the God of Light was among the most powerful.

"Among those, and other powers, he could also traverse the land as if he were light itself," Gregory added as he held the object up in his hand. "Behold, a teleportation totem."

The stone carved figure had lines that crisscrossed and patterned along its sides. Great detail was taken into account in the design of the runic artifact.

"It, too, has been inert for some time. Not that it would do me any good if it were energized. Mastery of such complex uses of mana is better suited to greater minds and more skilled disciples." Gregory gave a small smile.

So it was true what was written in the books of mana. Seelios was skeptical about the concept of a flowing energy in all things, living and non, but fascinated nonetheless. It was said that mana grants vitality, and being able to harbor such enormous amounts of it and manipulate it by will is what gives the gods their power. To hear Gregory speak of artifacts using mana seems to confirm the writings. Runic artifacts, after all, contained the power of the gods.

"Perhaps you will make better use of this than I." Gregory extended the teleportation totem out to Seelios and he slowly took it, marveling at the generous gift. A third runic artifact. His head was spinning. If his leg wasn't broken, he would've been jumping with excitement.

"Gods be good, I don't know what to say. Thank you," Seelios said as he looked at the intricate detail.

"I impart these gifts to you, but you should know that

such wonderful things can be deadly. If you call upon their power when you are too weak, they will end you."

Gregory pointed to Seelios's ring. "Even prolonged use of a truth ring can leave you feeble. If you go too far, it can kill you, leaving you with so little vitality that your heart won't have the strength to keep you alive."

Seelios looked down at the band on his finger. So that was its true name. He remembered being winded the few times he'd used the ring but always thought it was from the exhilaration and excitement. He swallowed nervously and nodded. "I understand."

Gregory nodded, seeming satisfied of his short lesson. He looked around the forest. "We best be going. The longer we stay in one spot, the more vulnerable we are."

When the night came, they reluctantly set up camp within the cover of thick brush to try to conceal themselves as much as they could. Bugs and ticks would be the least of their worries if they were found by minions of the God of Earth. A campfire would've stood out in the surrounding darkness, so they braved the night shivering under what little blankets and cloth they brought with them.

Dawn broke and Seelios expected to wake rested and energized. That hope was gone when his lids lifted as if the weight of the world were trying to hold them down. When he moved, his leg pained him even more than the previous day. It felt hot as a furnace, and a burning sensation spread from the center of his shin. Even through the thick bandages a smell of death came from the wound. His head was cloudy with strange thoughts, a hallucinatory state that seemed to be something more than just sleep deprivation.

His hand clutched the stone that the disciple had given him, as if he were clinging onto hope that a mere object might restore him overnight. He released his grip and saw sweat marks on it, despite feeling like he was frozen.

Gregory was already up and packing the few materials they had.

"My leg . . . it's worse than just a break, isn't it?" Seelios asked Gregory.

Gregory pursed his lips. "I'm no healer." He hesitated for a moment, as if considering whether or not he should continue. "Your bone punctured your skin. I dressed it as best I could, but if there's any hope for your survival we must reach town as soon as possible."

Seelios knew of such wounds before. Once the fever took from such an injury, there was little hope. Men had died in Fembleton with wounds less severe than Seelios's. Gregory eyed him, as if to judge how Seelios would react.

Seelios pushed himself up with arms that barely had strength within them. He tried his best to ignore the pain that told him to stop moving and lie there, collapsed on the forest floor. When he got to one knee, he was out of breath and drenched in sweat.

Seelios faced Gregory with a look of pain and determination. "Let's go."

7

The remainder of the hike to Alnerwick required the assistance of Gregory and a sturdy branch as a walking stick.

Trails of smoke were beginning to appear in the distance, a sign of civilization on the horizon. By the time the Alnerwick farmhouses came into view, Seelios was beginning to see bright spots of light. He smiled listlessly into the air as he chased them with his hands, oblivious to the arrival at their destination. He didn't even flinch at the heavy scent of manure as he plodded through the thick of it, spread over top the farmland.

Gregory asked something, but Seelios couldn't find the focus to respond. An overwhelming fog overtook his mind and he couldn't manage a single coherent thought. Seelios clutched at his chest as he felt his heart rate surge. He dropped his arm from around Gregory's shoulders and pulled at his shirt, trying to take it off in a flurry of madness as if the cloth were ablaze.

Gregory said something in reply. The world spun, and

Seelios lost all function in his legs. He would've fallen hard had it not been for Gregory, who eased Seelios gently to the ground. He stared up at the blue sky with its wispy clouds and couldn't tell if the lights in his vision were part of the sky or not, but everything seemed to swirl around the Daylight Star. His eyes struggled to focus as he gazed, and he drifted toward a deep and heavy sleep. Muffled shouts came from a distance, and the dark shapes of heads appeared around him.

Just as Seelios closed his eyes, his hand found its way into his pocket and seized the rejuvenation stone. In the midst of hallucination and pain, something inside told him to clutch the artifact for dear life.

WHEN SEELIOS WOKE, he found himself enveloped in a swaddle of thick blankets. He blinked at the wooden rafters above, his mind feeling much sharper than before. Despite this, he felt exhausted to a point where he questioned whether he'd be able to move. His neck was sore, pleading him to keep his head still, but his curiosity got the best of him. He braved the throbbing ache and slowly turned his face to take in his surroundings. The room was small and simple. He was on a bed pushed into the corner, his feet pointed at the door. There was a wooden desk and chair against the wall to his right, underneath a window that revealed a clear blue sky.

Seelios jumped when he saw the figure of a man sitting beside the desk. The motion sent a shiver of intense pain radiating from his leg.

"You scared me half to death," Seelios said, wincing.

Gregory gave a chuckle. "I scared you?" he said with

inflection. "I believe it hardly compares to what you put me through. We all thought you wouldn't make it through that first night."

The exhaustion of Seelios's muscles forced him to lie back down. "What happened?"

"It would appear your body refuses to let death get the better of you." Gregory smirked. "Or perhaps the God of Light." He nodded toward Seelios's hand.

Seelios shifted his head and saw that he clutched the rejuvenation stone. He brought it up to his face and saw the faintest trace of glowing runes etched onto its surface. The artifact was no longer just a cold smooth stone, but alive and pulsating with a small aura of energy.

"The sacred glyphs of Ophanim sparkle upon its surface. Such a glorious sight to see its power returned." Gregory smiled brightly.

"But how?" Seelios asked with a mystified look.

"In your brush with death you activated the artifact and used its power to mend your leg. Not entirely, I should say, but enough to drive away the infection and stop most of the bleeding." Gregory's smile faded. "But I'm afraid your leg still isn't well enough to travel."

Seelios looked down at the artifact. "Can't I use this to finish the healing?"

Gregory shook his head. "You've already used much of your own mana. You would risk death to mend a bone? Here, give it to me," Gregory said as he beckoned with his hand.

That explained why his body felt so tired. Seelios handed over the stone.

Gregory took the artifact in his hands and closed his eyes. Color seemed to drain from his face as his brow furrowed in concentration. Droplets of sweat streaked down from his forehead, wetting the neckline of his robe. He slumped forward and let out a long, laborious breath. "Here," he whispered as he held up the stone with a shaking hand. "Take it."

Seelios took the rejuvenation stone back and felt a noticeable warmth, as if it'd sat in the sun all day. The lines of light now twinkled with a distinct brightness much stronger than before.

Gregory sat back in his chair, chest heaving up and down as if he'd sprinted a mile. His eyes were half open and his face looked pained. "I hope that it is enough."

Seelios looked from the stone, then to Gregory with a face of concern. "What have you done? You look ill."

The disciple took a moment to still his breath to an even pace. "I'd heal you myself, but you appear to be much more skilled with the thing than I. I gave the stone a bit of my own mana so that you may use it."

"But you look as if you can barely keep yourself together. We could've waited until I was stronger."

Gregory turned his head toward the door and narrowed his eyes. He reached into his robes and produced something that looked like a small metal scroll fashioned with a large glass orb at the end. Shiny strips of orichalcum swirled and curved over the sphere's surface, meeting at the top. It emanated a terrible power that intimidated Seelios to his core.

"What you have in your hand . . . that's the runic artifact you used to attack the God of Earth?" Seelios asked.

"Indeed, the Lumastra. Never use it unless you've been properly trained," Gregory said, his eyes still focused on the door. He leaned forward as if he were straining to hear something.

Seelios tried to listen, but heard nothing. "What is it?"

"We must escape. I've too little strength to focus my senses, but I believe we may be in danger."

A forceful knock at the door made Seelios jump.

8
_____

"This is your last warning," an angry man said from the other side. "If you don't leave, we'll be forced to remove you ourselves."

Gregory stood up on unsteady legs and straightened his robes. "We?"

There was a moment of hesitant silence, followed by the incomprehensible grumbling of men talking.

"I'm here with four others, well-armed. If your boarding debt can't be paid, you'll be imprisoned."

Seelios looked from the door to Gregory with concern. "What debt?"

"We've been here for three days now and only had the coin for one. I could tell them of my courtly position at Paloise and be extended a bit of credit but, given the circumstances, I think we want as few people as possible to know who we are."

"Three days?" Seelios nearly shouted. "I've been asleep for that long?"

Gregory pursed his lips. "Consider yourself lucky. No one survives an infection the likes of which you suffered."

Another knock came, even louder than before.

"I can hear your muttering about in there. You best not be standing at the door when we break it down!" the angry voice said.

"Is this the danger you sensed?" Seelios asked.

Gregory watched the door with suspicion in his eye, holding out the wand-like object level in his hand. "Only peril seems to await on the other side. What do you propose we do?" Gregory turned with an expectant look.

"You're asking me?" Seelios asked, dumbfounded.

Seelios jumped at the noise of something hard striking the other side of their door.

A muffled voice said to another, "Have some care you brute. I'd like the frame intact."

Light sparked to life within the orb of the Lumastra and runes appeared down the orichalcum bands. If a decision wasn't made, Gregory would blast whomever came charging through that door.

Another loud bang came and a few splinters of wood fanned out from a bulge in the center.

Seelios's thoughts were racing. If only there were a way to get a sense of how dangerous the innkeep and his men were. Realization came, and he slipped off his ring. Without even having to close his eyes, the runes sparked to life with a certain eagerness, as if it were waiting to be noticed. It was a surreal experience using the artifact ring. When activated, it turned into a ghostly window that revealed the world in a different, truer light. He brought the ring to his eye and looked through the wispy cloud that fluttered inside the band. Through it, he saw the silhouetted shapes of two men standing at the door. One was hefting a large object with two hands while the other stood by. They had auras that flickered with a light shade of gray. There were uncertainties about them, but nothing about their energies said they were overtly evil. As far as men were concerned, they were likely good natured and had some of the closest auras to pure white he'd ever seen.

Seelios lowered the ring from his eye and the runes faded away from its surface. He felt his heart go shallow and breath draw short, the last bit of his energy seemingly used up from the artifact.

Gregory looked at him with concern. "I tried to warn you. You're likely within an inch of your life now, as if you had any vitality to spare. Perhaps you'll believe me when I tell you these things."

Seelios gave a tired nod, perspiration dripping off his blond hair and down his face. He looked back toward the door. "I think we should reason with them. They don't seem to be dangerous."

Gregory looked uncertain for a moment, but nodded and withdrew his weapon of light back into the sleeve of his robes.

Another loud bang at the door bulged the door even further. Movement could be seen in between cracks that had formed between the planks. Two more good hits and they'd be able to reach through and open the door themselves.

"We best not keep them waiting then." Gregory walked over and unlatched the iron bolts. He stepped aside just as the ram struck again, causing the door to swing open so violently that it crashed into the wall.

Standing in the doorway was a large man with a thick log wrapped in chains. He let it drop to the floor with a thunk and reached for his sword.

A smaller, middle-aged man stepped into view. "Finally came to your senses? Would've preferred you open the door the first time." The man looked at Seelios for a moment and narrowed his eyes. "Don't think that I'm fooled by your mockeries," he said as he gestured toward Seelios's leg.

Seelios looked down at the bed, then back up. "Pardon?"

The innkeeper ignored Seelios and threw a seething look at Gregory. "I need the three golds I'm owed and for the lot of you to leave this town for good." He glanced at the door, barely hanging on its hinges as if it were charged by a large bull. "Make that six golds and five silvers."

"We don't have any more money," Seelios said. "But I'm sure we can—"

The innkeeper spat onto the floor and raised a finger. "You listen here and you listen good, boy. Hurt or not, you don't come and take advantage of the folk of this town, lurking about and causing a ruckus at night!"

Seelios and Gregory exchanged confused looks.

Gregory put up his hands in an appeasing manner. "Walter, there must be some misunderstanding. Aside from our shortcomings in paying you, I can assure that we haven't been been causing any—"

"Don't you say it. Don't you dare!" Walter shook an angry finger at Gregory. "I won't stand here and be lied to by the likes of you and your strange lookin' eyes! After all the hospitality my family and I have shown you. I've seen the both of you, yes even you, boy, wandering about." He walked up to Gregory and shoved the finger in his face. "You have the nerve to lie to me like this? After I chased you over here from the trees by my house?"

"By your house? I've been nowhere but this very room all day," Gregory said.

Gregory looked up, thoughtful for a moment, then his eyes widened in a look of terror-filled realization.

"What is it?" Seelios asked.

Gregory looked back up to the innkeeper. "When you saw us, can you describe what we looked like?"

Walter smirked and crossed his arms. "I can say this; you're good. How you managed to get here and get so cleaned up after being filthy from head to toe is a mystery to me. Damn near look like you rolled around in the dirt road. Where did you stash those muddy robes? If they're dirtying any of my fine linens I'll be having you pay for that, too!"

Seelios looked at Gregory and realized his perception of danger was misguided, but real.

Seelios turned to Walter. "Everyone needs to leave town."

This only seemed to enrage the innkeeper further. "Don't think that sort of trickery will work on me, boy. You lot may have swindled every honest businessman across Inf before you got here, but the fun—"

A cry came out from the larger man outside the room. "Gods be good. You snuck up on me!" His head was turned down the hallway. "You, but wait, how can—" He looked at Gregory with bewilderment, then back down the hall. "Do you have a twin brother?"

Walter turned his head to look over his shoulder. "Well? Who is it?"

"It—it's him!" The larger man pointed at Gregory. "Except . . . ."

Walter gave a huff and stomped out into the hallway with a look of annoyance. His face dropped to disbelief and grew pale, doing a double take with Gregory's face.

The larger man raised his sword but something that resembled an arm knocked it away, sending it sliding across the wood out of view.

"Gregory," Seelios whispered with a slight quiver in his voice.

The old disciple nodded as he pulled out the Lumastra from his sleeve.

Walter began backing into the room with Seelios and Gregory. "H—hey now. We don't want any trouble from you."

A tall cloaked figure stepped through the doorway, crouching down to avoid hitting the frame. It leered around the room with wide eyes that didn't appear to have lids. Its chin was long and misshapen on one side and had almost nothing for a mouth. It had white hair and a beard trim similar to Gregory's. It was a figure that seemed hastily made to resemble a human, but clearly missed the mark. Its visage was locked into a perpetual look of surprise and hunger, near terrifying to make eye contact with.

Seelios tried to squeak out to Gregory to attack, but fear rendered his vocal cords silent.

"You confuse me with this monstrosity, Walter? Surely you think I'm more attractive than this foul thing."

It shambled toward them, scraping along the wood floor. Walter ducked out of the way, screaming, as a blast of light sent the monster flying in a ball of flame. It hit the wall with a heavy thud and crumbled to the floor to the sound of a small landslide. It lay at the foot of Seelios's bed in a pile of charred and melting mud. Bits of burning robe and chunks of earth were scattered about the room and scorched holes into the bed sheets.

Gregory snatched the bedding and battered the flames of the clay man's remains until they were extinguished. A misshapen arm reached up from the amorphous pile, prompting Gregory to give it a swift kick and shower a screaming Walter with clumps of mud.

"Now you believe us, I assume?" Gregory asked Walter.

Walter crouched in the corner, panting. He looked up to Gregory and nodded as he wiped spots of dirt from his face.

"Good, then help me with Seelios," Gregory said.

"What was that thing?" Walter asked as he stood up, looking down at the burnt remains of the clay man.

"Something sent by the God of Earth," Seelios said.

"God of Earth? But, we've done nothing." Walter frowned, then brightened as he looked at Gregory. "But you could help us! You could use that thing of yours."

Gregory shook his head. "If he comes, I would only be able to delay him. Everyone must leave before it's too late." He gestured toward Seelios's legs. "Can you move?"

"I think so," Seelios said as he flexed his knee. It felt weak, but the pain was gone. It took all of Seelios's strength to get off the bed. His leg was wrapped in fresh bandages and splinted on both sides with wide pieces of wood. He slowly stood on his good leg, steadying himself on the nightstand. The motion took so much effort that his shaking body nearly knocked over a flower vase in the process. The pain was nauseating and he began to sway. Walter and Gregory ran to his side and braced him before he fell.

"Easy there, boy." Gregory threw Seelios's arm over his own shoulders.

"Thank you," Seelios said.

They began to walk across the room together, but something compelled Seelios to stop. "Wait." Seelios looked back at the night stand. "We might need that."

Gregory gave him a peculiar look. Seelios hopped over and grabbed the vase, leaving the wet flower stem on the night stand.

The three of them hobbled down the end of the hallway and found a group of curious onlookers gathered at the bottom of the staircase. The debacle must've created quite the ruckus and attracted the attention of folks from the bar area on the first floor. The crowd parted when Seelios reached the bottom step with the help of Gregory and Walter.

The tap room looked similar to the Withertree, just only about half the size. The bar was in the corner with but a few stools, occupied by two men and a mustached bartender. A small scattering of tables held a mixture of traveling merchants and local villagers. Almost ever single eye in the room was staring at the three of them.

"This town is in great danger. You must leave immediately," Gregory said to the crowd.

The villagers' reactions were confused and unsure, looking to each other for clues of understanding. They began to whisper among themselves and throw suspicious looks, eying the sun emblem on Gregory's chest.

"Listen to the man, he speaks the truth!" Walter said.

Seelios saw a hooded figure rise out of a seat. Gripping the neck of the flower vase, he watched the figure clamber toward them. Gregory pulled out the Lumastra, ready to fire another beam, when Seelios sloshed the figure with the vase water. The man reeled back and threw off his hood in the process, showing a misshapen face that looked like Seelios. It stumbled, clutching at its cheek. When it pulled its hand away, half of its face fell off and broke apart in clumps on the floor.

Half of the tavern was on their feet and backing away from the scene. Some drew swords while others looked on with fear and confusion.

"Well done," Gregory said as he stashed away his weapon.

Another hooded figure stood from one of the tables and raced out the door.

Seelios cursed beneath his breath.

"My wife and child, I must go to them," Walter said.

"Go. Take them away from here and keep them safe," Gregory said as he threw Seelios's arm back over his shoulders.

Walter ran out, following the stream of panicked people that were exiting the bar.

9

Seelios and Gregory emerged from the tavern into Alnerwick's village square, a patch of hard packed earth that centered around a stone brick well. Most of the village's shops and homes surrounded the plaza with a few more huts scattered through the neighboring farmlands.

The ground began to shake and large cracks formed in the earth.

Gregory pulled the Lumastra from his sleeve. "Go to Paloise and find the other disciples."

"I can't just leave you—"

"Go now, boy! Use the stone to mend your leg and run."

The shaking of the earth grew more violent as the cracks widened into deep fissures. Panicked villagers fled their homes and filled the streets.

Seelios focused his mind on the rejuvenation stone and felt it grow hot in response. The mana from the artifact leeched into his hand and flowed through his body like a river of sunlight. Strength returned to his injured leg as he felt his bone reattach and solidify. Use of the artifact was surprisingly effortless, even enjoyable, but the charged mana within it was quickly depleted. He let his mind release before it began to sap his own vitality, praying that it had been enough to mend him whole. He worked to decouple the splint and unwrap the bandages, revealing the raw pink skin beneath. A large, textured scar drew a vertical line down his left shin.

Green light glowed through the cracks in the earth as an armored figure emerged out of the ground atop a rising column of rock, wielding a familiar rune-lit axe. A black scorch mark streaked across his face, making his enraged visage even more intimidating.

Gregory raised the Lumastra and light began to gather within the orb. A boulder burst from the dirt beneath his feet and sent the disciple tumbling through the air, robes flapping wildly as he soared. He crashed through a wooden post that held up a shop's awning and the light within the Lumastra dissipated. Blue canvas sagged to one side, hovering just over Gregory as he lay on the deck, unmoving.

A hearty laugh boomed, echoing off the buildings. "It's a pity to see one endowed with such power, yet still so weak and fragile." The God of Earth leapt down from the column with a thunderous shake. His strides sent tremors through the ground with each step.

Seelios circled the boulder as lines of green light began tracing over its surface.

"Seelios," Gregory said, his eyes wrought with pain. "I told you to run." He looked over Seelios's shoulder with concern.

"The totem is your last hope. You must awaken it if you're to escape," Gregory said.

"I can't just leave you here like this," Seelios said.

"Your life is far more important than mine. Go, find the other disciples. Tell them who you are."

Seelios's mind raced with panic and fear. He reached inside his pocket and grasped the teleportation totem. He tried to connect with it, but it was as if he were stumbling around in the dark of a strange room. He pushed harder to drown out the noise around him, and then he found it. A familiar ping of emotion came, as if he rediscovered something that was thought to be lost long ago. An intense exhaustion spread through his body, the little mana he had left draining away to the hunger of the sleeping artifact. The icy touch of death prodded at his vulnerable heart, making every beat weaker than the last.

The hard fingers of the golem wrapped around Seelios and lifted him through the awning of the shop in an explosion of wood splinters and ripping fabric. Seelios struggled in the stony grip, dizziness taking over as the golem squeezed. He looked up at the sun blazing in the sky, expecting it to be the last thing he saw before being crushed to death. In his gaze, Seelios felt the sun speak to him. It didn't communicate with words, but conveyed a certain feeling of realization, like an awakening of something that he already knew. He heard the familiar sound of his father's voice.

The crisp blue sky began to darken above and fade to a dusk hue. The bright disk of the sun was reduced to a mere glow, as if a heavy fog drifted in. On that sunny day, the entire town of Alnerwick was shrouded in a moment of enchanting darkness. If the people looked far enough, they could see traces of a blue sky only at the horizon.

Seelios felt the warmth of the borrowed daylight enter his body and surround him, giving him a surge of vitality and power. He funneled it through his arm and into the totem. Beams of light shot from between the stone fingers that wrapped around Seelios.

"Think of a place, any place other than here!" Gregory shouted with a raspy voice.

Seelios's blurred vision was replaced by something else. He suddenly saw himself as a young child again, being carried away down the river in a homemade boat. He saw the clearing where Garrick and his father found him. The world around him melted away into blinding light, and he felt himself weightless, soaring through the air. The light disappeared, and a forest floor rushed up at him. The ground met him with a violent impact and darkness came.

10

Three days of hard riding on the road wasn't something Garrick was used to, doubly so without any provisions or proper travel equipment. Shortly after their flight from Fembleton, Garrick and Emeline thought it best to stay off the Trade Road and keep to the woods. Though their journey would've been considerably longer, it felt safer.

Garrick attempted to snare animals to compensate for their lack of provisions, but with the blight scouring the lands, there weren't too many animals in sight. They must have all fled to richer lands in the north where food grew in bountiful amounts. Garrick's father used to say if they were ever in danger of starvation they could just travel to the northern water lands where the feasts were endless and the markets were plentiful. The blight also made it difficult to find edible herbs and mushrooms along the way, but Emeline didn't let that stop her. It was odd that, despite the stories of the blight only being localized to Fembleton, they seemed to discover it wherever they went.

In any other circumstance, it would've been Garrick's

dream to have so much time alone with Emeline; however, weary days turned into weary nights, and during a time of sorrow and grief, Garrick couldn't find the courage to court her. Although, there were times Garrick swore Emeline didn't seem to mind being with him. She held him tighter than necessary when riding, and one particular night she pressed close against him by the fire. Still, Garrick convinced himself that she was just cold and needed the extra warmth, nothing more.

Barely any words were spoken when they left Fembleton, just muted silence and the occasional physical touch that sent Garrick's heart aflutter. It was almost enough to distract him from his insatiable thirst for ale.

They galloped through the forest, sure to keep the river in sight as it was their only guide. The closest place that Garrick could think to be safe was Paloise, as long as it wasn't overrun with murderous rock creatures by the time they arrived. If Paloise had fallen, they could find shelter in another small village in the countryside, but they would be no more protected than they were in Fembleton. There was nowhere else to go unless Acorn grew a pair of wings and could carry them far away to another god's territory, save for the Kingdom of Zelerum, the God of Earth's domain.

The canopy of the forest grew thin, and they emerged into a small clearing off the side of the river. Garrick's breath drew short when he recognized the place. It was the same clearing where he and Ricker saved Seelios. He stopped Acorn and lingered at the tree line, taking in the place in its entirety. He looked out to the river and pictured a younger Seelios peeking over the edge of his boat, eyes filled with terror. Sadness came as Garrick thought of Seelios taken away by the rock monster in Fembleton.

Garrick stood in the saddle and squinted at something

laying in front of them on the river bank. A man in traveler's robes lay face down in the sand, feet still in the shallows of the river as it lapped around his ankles. His arm appeared to clutch a sack bulging with its contents. The stringy white hair was unmistakable.

"Fancy a wager as to who that man might be?" Garrick said.

Emeline squinted into the distance and gasped. "I'm surprised that wretch made it this far."

"What happened back in Fembleton, he had something to do with it. How else would a man know to leave with such urgency?" Garrick sat back down in the saddle and trotted Acorn into the clearing, keeping a safe distance. He lifted his leg over the saddle and lowered himself to the ground.

Cassius was sprawled on his stomach, sand covering his face. A wooden oar lay beside him.

Garrick looked downriver and saw a boat bobbing up and down, stuck against two rocks that jutted out of the water. The river foamed and rushed in a dangerous rapid, the same rapid that threatened Seelios's life years ago.

Seelios had been right. The weight of all that coin probably made it too difficult to navigate the river properly. Cassius must've got thrown from his boat and tried to swim to shore, still hefting his oversized purse. It was amazing that he'd even made it to shore with all that weight.

"Do you think he's still alive?" Emeline called out from atop Acorn.

Garrick shrugged. "I know of a method that's worked with me in the past."

He stood next to Cassius and gave him a hard shove with his foot. The old innkeep rolled onto his back as his arm flopped onto the sand, revealing a glistening crystal that hung from a leather cord around his neck.

Acorn reared into the air and gave a terrified cry. Emeline screamed as she slide from the saddle and landed on the soft dirt. The horse pranced around, eyes wild with panic and fear. It made a series of motions that looked like it was desperate to get away, like the crazed dance of an animal that had suddenly gone mad. The horse turned and galloped toward the trees, back in the direction of Fembleton.

"Acorn!" Garrick yelled, running after her, but it was no use. Before Garrick took three steps she had already disappeared through the foliage.

He ran after her and continued to yell her name and whistle through his fingers. It wasn't long before he could no longer hear the frantic pace of the horse racing through the leaves and brush.

He came back into the clearing and walked up to Emeline. "Are you hurt?"

"I don't think so," Emeline said, brushing sand off her arms and green dress. She ran her fingers through her thick, red hair and tried to shake out what she could.

"Shit of a whore," Garrick said through gritted teeth, glancing back to the trees. "Acorn was our only hope getting to Paloise. Gods be damned!" he yelled, kicking at the sand.

Garrick yanked his sword out of its scabbard and turned an angry eye toward Cassius. "Even as a carcass this blasted man causes grief." He stomped over and raised his blade into the air.

"Garrick, stop!" Emeline said.

"I'm going to hack this man into pieces and feed him to the fishes," Garrick said. His eyes became transfixed on the crystal necklace around Cassius's neck. It began to shine with a glowing red hue.

"Wh—what? No, you can't do that! We don't even know for sure that he's dead."

"Here's how I know for sure," Garrick said. He brought his foot back and kicked Cassius hard in the ribs, rolling him back onto his stomach.

Garrick thought he saw Cassius grimace. He waited for a moment, then decided he'd imagined it. He turned to Emeline. "Did you see him move? I didn't. Must be dead, and dead people don't need nice things."

Garrick bent down and searched Cassius's robes, desperately hoping to find a hidden flask. His heart jumped when his fingers felt something, but realized it was just the handle of a dagger. He was just about to give up and walk away when his eyes fell back to the crystal necklace in the sand. He stared at it for a moment, transfixed on the glistening jewel. It captivated him, pulling him deeper into its beautiful facets and, for a split second, he forgot where he was. He reached down and snapped it off Cassius's neck with a sharp yank.

Emeline walked up to Garrick and snatched the sword out of his hand.

"Calm down, I'll give it right back," Emeline said, just before Garrick was about to protest. Garrick pocketed the crystal and watched her walk around to the other side of Cassius.

Emeline polished a portion of the blade with her dress until it glinted in the sun. She squatted and brought the edge up underneath Cassius's nose. A faint cloud of moisture appeared on the surface of the metal.

"He's still alive," Emeline said, with an inflection of surprise. She stood and handed the sword back to Garrick.

"Great. What are we to do with an unconscious villain?" Garrick said.

"As much as it pains me to say this, we can't leave him. It's not right," Emeline said with a frown.

"You must be jesting with me. Can you be serious?" Garrick made a look of disgust. "This man has treated you, me, and everyone else in Fembleton like filth our whole lives."

"I know." Emeline looked at Garrick. "But we'd be no better than the monsters that attacked our village if we left someone to die out here."

Garrick turned away and scoffed. "If it were up to me I'd remove his head and mount it on the tavern wall."

Emeline looked at Garrick with concern in her eyes. "I've never heard you so angry and resentful before. You should be careful before those feelings consume you."

"Perhaps they already have," Garrick said.

A tense moment of silence passed between them.

Emeline shifted uncomfortably in her stance and looked to the trees. "What are we to do now that Acorn has left us?"

Garrick pointed downriver. "The boat that Cassius was traveling in; if I can free it from those rocks, we may be able to use it."

Garrick grabbed the oar next to Cassius and made his way along the bank. He searched for the least treacherous path of exposed river rocks that led through the rapids.

Water splashed and foamed around his legs as he carefully waded into the turbulent waters. He kept his knees bent and his arms outstretched, pulse pounding with fear as he thought about the danger he was putting himself in. One slip and he would be swept down river, carried away to his death.

Garrick slid his foot forward along the river bed, feeling around with his foot to find a good place to hold before he shifted his weight. He wedged a foot, but as he began to move forward his balance shifted. He flailed the oar in his hand as the churning water threatened to take him down.

A cry came from behind Garrick. "Be careful!" Emeline said.

Garrick turned and saw her standing at the bank. Her brow was furrowed with concern and she fidgeted nervously with her hands. He flashed his best reassuring smile and turned back to the boat, just a few steps away. Water surged around the larger rocks that trapped the vessel on its side. Garrick just hoped it wasn't damaged beyond repair. He inched closer, grabbed a jagged rock edge and managed to get a foothold without slipping. Rushing water tugged at his pants as he pulled himself out of the river. He stood triumphant, looking down at the water coursing around him. Just below his feet, the hull of Cassius's boat scraped noisily against the stone.

It was one of Fembleton's small fishing vessels, built to float around their lake as more of a leisure activity than a means of traveling across Inf. Despite it's design, it appeared to have suffered only minor scratches on the wood surface, from what Garrick could see. With the way the current trapped it against the rock, it was half submerged in the water. Garrick was concerned for the hull portion that wasn't visible.

Using the oar as best as he could, he pried the boat to turn it right side up. The oar bent, threatening to crack, but managed to tilt the boat enough for the water to take hold of it and twist its position until it was completely upside down. It wasn't the end goal Garrick had in mind, but at least it was a step in the right direction. He pressed again with the oar, but only managed to push it away from the rock. It started drifting as the current took hold once more. A loud groan echoed off the trees while the wooden hull slid across wet stone.

Garrick cursed as he dashed to the other side of the rock and, oar in hand, jumped into the river with a splash. When he surfaced, he nearly took the boat's bow directly to his forehead. Emeline screamed as he jerked out of the way and the boat slid by him, brushing against his cheek. He choked on foaming water that splashed his face. His vision was blurred from river water stinging his eyes, but he managed to get a hold of a wooden edge before the boat slipped past him. He braced the oar against its side and forced it right-side up. His muscles strained as he hoisted himself into the boat, nearly capsizing it in the process. He landed with a sloppy thud in a tangled mess of waterlogged rope and fishing nets.

Speeding down the river, Garrick sat himself upright and used the oar to paddle toward the shore. He felt the boat scrape against the rocks of the shallows when he drew near the bank. Emeline came high-stepping into the river with a face scrunched up in fury and concern.

"You scared me half to death! Why in heavens would you jump like that?" Emeline asked. She glared at him as she grabbed the side of the boat.

"We were going to lose it," Garrick said as he jumped down with a splash. "If I hadn't leapt after it, the current would've taken it to Paloise without us in it."

Emeline pursed her lips and shook her head. "You nearly died. You would've left me all alone out here. Is that what you want?"

"No, of course—"

"Then think of me before you do that again!" Emeline's lip quivered and she looked away.

"I . . . I'm sorry," Garrick said.

They pulled the boat through the sand, the silence broken only by the occasional strained grunt. By the time they reached the clearing, Garrick's back and arms ached like he'd been working the fields all day.

Slumping down onto the ground to catch his breath, he looked over to Emeline. "Thank you."

Emeline threw him a sideways glance. "It's not like I was going to let you pull that all by yourself," she mumbled.

"No. I mean, thank you for that, but also thank you for earlier."

Emeline raised an eyebrow.

Garrick looked over at Cassius's body. "I don't know what came over me then. Sometimes I don't feel like myself. But you . . . ." He looked at Emeline, who had turned to face him. "You help me remember what it's like to be a good person."

A small smile spread across Emeline's lips and she brushed a lock of red hair out of her face.

"Not just now, but always. My life has been difficult, and I fear it's only become worse. But when I'm with you I forget all that."

Emeline drew in a breath, her smile widening. "I'm glad."

Garrick looked at Emeline with his own smile. Despite just fleeing the massacre of their home village and having pulled a boat through a hundred feet of sand, she still looked as radiant as ever. He didn't know what he would do without her.

Emeline looked down sheepishly. "Garrick, you're staring."

Garrick blinked and looked away. "Terribly sorry."

He brushed himself off and stood. He looked back over to the boat. "Right, so our stolen vessel."

"Borrowed," Emeline said, playfully.

"Borrowed," Garrick said, smiling at her. "We need to make sure it wasn't damaged. It worked well enough in the short trip to shore, but it must stay afloat."

Emeline cleared her throat and straightened up. "Yes, of course," she said in a deep, mocking voice. "Serious business these boat affairs."

Garrick gave her a look, and they both laughed. It had been so long since Garrick felt relaxed. He looked at Emeline's smiling face and realized that the world would be a dark place if it wasn't for her and, one day, he would tell her how he truly felt.

Garrick looked at the boat and noticed the canvas cushioning sewn into the sides, the work of Fembleton's tailor. Tied against the cushions were various packs of supplies and clothing. It was no wonder the boat was so hard to right in the water, there was enough to last a journey to Paloise almost twice over. Cassius wasn't just taking a short visit, he'd provisioned himself for the span of months, possibly never to return.

"That scum knew the attack was going to happen," Garrick said with a frown. "He must've. How else would one know to prepare like this?" He turned to Emeline.

Emeline shook her head. "But how? Why wouldn't he have told anyone else?"

Garrick pushed the boat and rolled it upside-down so the hull faced the sky. He brushed off the caked sand and cursed.

"What is it?" Emeline asked, hovering over his shoulder.

"Exactly what I was afraid of. The hull's cracked." Garrick pointed to two spots where chunks of wood had broken off, revealing wide enough gaps to squeeze two fingers through.

Emeline furrowed her brow. "Those aren't too big. Isn't there something we can do to patch it?"

Garrick stood and thought for a moment. He looked down at his sword, then toward the trees. "We can use tree sap."

CHOPPING a hole into a tree was the easy part, as Garrick was lucky enough to have tools somewhat appropriate for the job; however, collecting the sap and treating it was another story.

Eager not to waste any more time, they fixed several flat river stones together by piling them into a makeshift container to hold the sap. They left a space underneath for a fire and mixed the sap in with some clay to make a paste. The heat made the sap thick and sticky, causing it to bubble and hiss. Emeline drew up a dab with a long stick, and it stretched up like a heavy piece of melted cheese.

"How did you learn this?" Emeline said, staring at the glistening brown strand until it finally separated.

Garrick sat back and smiled into the fire crackling under the pile of stones.

"Father taught me on the farm when I was young. A way to mend woodwork in a pinch," he said. He gave a soft chuckle. "I mocked that I'd never make use of the lesson."

The smile on Garrick's face lingered for a moment before it faded to a sad and distant stare. "I miss them."

Silence passed between Emeline and Garrick.

He looked at Emeline. "My parents, that is." He looked back down at the fire. "Decades have passed since they were killed, but it's just . . . I wish I'd more time with them."

In the stew of sadness he felt a flicker of something else inside, something that reminded him of his nightmares. He was suddenly aware of the crystal hidden in his pocket. His hand went to it and he felt a jolt of something dreadful inside his soul when his fingers touched its jagged surface.

"It must be lonely for you on that farm," Emeline said.

Garrick let go of the crystal and withdrew his hand. "I wish I never inherited it. It's just a reminder of a family that was torn apart too soon. One of the reasons why I frequent the tavern so."

A shiver went through his body at the thought of drinking an ale, causing his mouth to go dry. Garrick had done his best to distract himself from his insatiable thirst since his flask emptied, but in that moment he would've given almost anything for just one more drop of the foaming amber liquid.

Emeline placed hand on Garrick's arm and the contact made him jump to his feet and back away.

"What's wrong?" Emeline asked.

Garrick looked down at her, just as shocked. "Sorry, I . . . ."

Emeline smiled. "That's alright, sit back down. The paste needs a bit more time."

"We'll need more. I'll fetch some," he said as he backed away from a confused looking Emeline.

Garrick hefted his sword as he walked back over to the trees, cursing himself for acting like such a fool. She was everything he'd always wanted, and now that they were alone he didn't know what to do with the intimacy. Flickers of strange emotions mixed in his chest; sadness, pain, anxiety, and there was something else. He still couldn't tell what it was, but it was growing.

The crystal beckoned for Garrick's touch, but he pushed it out of his mind and walked to the tree line of the clearing's edge. He stopped and stared at the ground, deep in thought. He had to do it, he had to tell Emeline everything. And not just about his feelings for her but about everything that was happening to him.

He leaned his hand against the trunk of an alder tree as he rehearsed what he was going to say in his head. When he turned away, he didn't notice the bruise of decay spreading on the tree from where his palm had just been.

"Weren't you getting more sap?" Emeline asked when Garrick returned.

"What?" He looked down at the sword he was holding, completely unused since their first sapping. He flushed with embarrassment.

"Must've forgotten," Garrick said as he sheathed the sword.

Emeline gave a confused look. Garrick opened his mouth to talk, but froze. Overwhelming nervousness rendered him wide-eyed and speechless, something that seemed to happen a lot in front of Emeline.

Eager to distract himself, he drew up some paste from their fire. The thick dark liquid looked like molasses, stubbornly clinging to the stick. It looked ready. He walked it over and painted the glob of sap onto the hull, spreading it around so it filled the crack.

Emeline stood, walked over, and placed a hand on his shoulder. "Garrick, are you well?"

Garrick took a deep breath and set down the stick. "I've something to tell you." The thought of sharing his nightmares with her was terrifying, but it helped to share it with Seelios in a moment of weakness. Perhaps with Emeline it would be similar.

She gave a smile and looked deep into his eyes. "Does this have anything to do with what you were going to say at the tavern?"

Garrick flushed crimson, surprised that she remembered. "I, well, no, I mean . . . I want to tell you that too."

He took in another deep breath. "The truth is," Garrick started. He shifted uncomfortably in his stance as Emeline stepped closer with an expectant look, forcing his gaze down in a bashful reaction. His heart pounded in his chest.

"The truth is I—" Garrick lifted his head, and his eyes went wide.

Two arms appeared from behind Emeline, one brandishing a dagger to her throat while the other clamped over a muffled scream.

"No!" Garrick yelled.

"Now, now. Stay back or someone might get hurt." Cassius bared his yellow and brown teeth in a wicked smile from behind Emeline's red hair.

11

"Cassius, if you don't unhand her right now I swear I'll end your life!" Garrick said.

"An interesting proposal; however, I decline your offer and have another instead. Hand over what you stole or it'll get messy for the wench."

Garrick shifted his eyes to Emeline, who stared back at him with a look of sheer terror. He wanted to save her, but found himself battling an overwhelming desire to keep the crystal. His hand went down to his pocket and fidgeted with the jewel, clutching it in a tight fist. Emeline's eyes darted down to his hand, then back up as if to beg him to comply.

Garrick straightened and swallowed nervously. "I don't know what you're talking about."

Emeline's eyes melted into tearful disbelief. The sadness and betrayal written on her face was so apparent that Garrick had to look away.

"You lie." Cassius pulled the knife closer to Emeline's throat and she gave another muffled scream.

Garrick watched a trickle of blood roll down her neck from where the knife bit. Emotions turmoiled inside him.

He knew what must be done, but struggled with all of his will to commit to action.

Emeline tried to yell something, but her voice came out in muted tones through Cassius's hand. Garrick caressed the sharp edges of the crystal in his pocket. He slowly drew it up with his hand and held it in the air, the ends of the broken leather cord trembling as they hung through his shaking fingers.

Cassius's eyes grew wide and hungry at the sight of the crystal. "Yes, that's it. Give it here."

"Release her first," Garrick said.

Cassius curled his lip into a sneer. "I know your desires. You yearn to keep the shard to yourself. Don't think I can't see past your treachery."

Garrick wanted to yell and call him a liar, but his words were true. He couldn't easily give the crystal up. Something drew him into its beautiful surface, something that Garrick didn't understand. One thing was clear, the longer he held the crystal, the more the nightmares began to make sense. The voice he remembered was no longer menacing and sinister, but had spoken truth and purpose. Suddenly, the voice came again in that moment in front of Cassius and Emeline. It told Garrick to do as Cassius said.

The crystal trembled in Garrick's outstretched shaking hand. Cassius inched closer, keeping his knife tight against Emeline. Half the neckline of her green dress was matted against her chest, soaked with blood. When he was within reach, he snatched the crystal out of Garrick's hand.

The moment Garrick felt the crystal leave his fingertips he felt like his heart had been ripped out. The pain was sudden and immediate, and he moved to grab it back.

"Don't you dare," Cassius said as he took a few steps backward, still holding the knife to Emeline.

"Cassius, you scumbag!" Emeline yelled, now free of Cassius's hand. "You got your necklace, now let us go."

"The crystal, give it back," Garrick said, in a pleading voice.

Emeline's face twisted into confusion and disbelief. "Garrick," she whispered.

Cassius lifted his eyes from the crystal that he held in his palm and gave a wicked smile. He dropped the knife from Emeline's throat and shoved her away.

Garrick made no motion to catch her as she stumbled in the sand and fell. He stepped over Emeline and walked toward Cassius with a certain hunger in his eyes.

Cassius clenched the crystal in his hands and drew back his arm, poised to throw it. "Take one more step and it goes into the river."

Garrick froze in his tracks. He could've easily overpowered Cassius, but the thought of losing the crystal brought him to a panic so deep that it felt like his heart would burst.

"Garrick, what are you doing? Let's just leave. You don't need that thing," Emeline said.

Cassius's brown and yellow teeth showed through his wide grin. Garrick desired the crystal beyond reason, and would do anything for it. The look in Cassius's eyes showed that he knew it too.

Cassius opened his palm and presented the gleaming crystal to Garrick. It sparkled in the sunlight, radiating a rainbow of colors like a magical diamond. Garrick's eyes watered at the sight of the thing. His lust for it was stronger than anything he'd ever felt. It was a longing that made his whole being ache.

"You want this, don't you?" Cassius said with a sneer. He moved his eyes to Emeline. "Kill her."

Garrick stood for a moment, still looking at the crystal. He watched as Cassius held it up and dangled it in the air.

"Kill her and it shall be yours," Cassius said.

Garrick's pulse quickened. The possibility of having the crystal back in his possession, holding it in his hands again, was intoxicating. He pulled his sword from its scabbard and turned toward Emeline.

"Garrick, no!" Emeline screamed as she took a step back.

In only two strides Garrick was within reach of Emeline. The moment his sword plunged into her torso, he felt his emotions change. The veil of excitement lifted, revealing the terrible thing he had just done. Emeline's eyes went wide as her fingers fumbled over the blade in her chest, shoved nearly all the way to its hilt. Garrick gaped with horror, looking down at the sword in his hand, then back up to her face. He backed away, his legs shaking and unresponsive. He fell onto the ground with his eyes still fixated on Emeline, skewered by his blade. She swayed on her feet, then collapsed.

"W—what have I done?" Garrick whispered with a quivering voice as he looked down at his blood soaked sleeve, nearly all white but moments before. He crawled over to her on his hands and knees.

She was lying on her side. The blade had pierced through her chest and protruded out her back, steel dripping red. She wheezed as she struggled to breathe.

"Garrick, I'm so cold," Emeline said, barely a whisper. The whites of her teeth were dark with blood that bubbled up from her throat.

"Gods be damned. We'll get you out of here. I'll get you to a healer," Garrick said with a panicked tone as he stripped off his green vest, then his shirt. The white cloth pooled dark red stains as he draped it over her with shaking hands.

"I won't make it." Her voice was barely audible.

Garrick's face twisted up as he struggled to fight back his anguish. Tears blurred his vision. "No. No no no no," Garrick said. He ran his fingers through his hair and began rocking back and forth.

Emeline slowly lifted a palm and rested it on his, looking into his eyes. "Hold my hand," she whispered.

Garrick looked with wavering eyes at her delicate, white skin. He turned his palm up and worked his fingers between hers, curling them around the back of her hand. She returned the gesture with a small squeeze. When he looked down at her, she stared back at him with pain, but still held a smile in her eyes.

"Emeline, I'm so sorry. I lost myself, I . . . please, I could never forgive myself if I lost you. Don't leave me."

"I forgive you." She tried taking another breath but instead turned her head and coughed up thick blood that spattered the ground. "But you must . . . forgive yourself."

Emeline raised her eyes, barely able to hold them open, and smiled. In the faintest whisper, she said, "I would've died hiding in that tavern." Her voice grew weaker with each word. "But you saved me. At least we had these last . . . moments."

Her hand went limp and slid out of his grip. Her eyelids drifted shut with her smile still lingering on her face.

"Emeline?" Garrick grabbed her by the shoulder and gave her a shake. "Emeline!" Her curly red hair slid over her face. He stared for a moment, waiting for her to say something.

"Emeline, you can't die. I need you." Garrick's words

nearly came out in sobs. He brushed her hair away to reveal her beauty. "I love you," he said with a shuddering voice.

Garrick shut his eyes and rested his head on her shoulder. Tears streamed out and soaked the bloody shirt that draped over her. Garrick lifted his head and gave an anguished cry, tears of rage streaking down his cheeks. Unfathomable anger coursed through his veins.

Garrick stood and spun around, wiping his eyes. The spot where Cassius once stood had nothing but bare silt and sand. "Where have you fled, coward?" Garrick screamed. His eyes swept the clearing and saw the boat was gone. He walked to where it was dragged into the river and saw a sparkle in the sand.

Garrick stared at the crystal for a moment, all the feelings of rage and anguish slowly drained out of him. He bent down and picked it up. Something sinister spread through him, replacing his old anger with a new one. It was a type of anger that he only felt in the smallest echoes of his nightmares.

A voice came to him inside his head as clear as if it had been whispered into his ear.

"Welcome to the wretched," the voice of his nightmares said.

Garrick tied the leather cord around his neck and let the crystal hang against his bare chest, his once anguished face now solemn and emotionless. He turned away from the river and walked past Emeline's body, into the woods.

12

S eelios groaned as he rolled over and felt the knots of tree roots under his back. He opened his eyes and saw sunlight peering through a canopy of leaves overhead.

"Gregory!" Seelios shouted as he sat up. The motion caused excruciating pain in the side of his chest, and he lay back on the ground.

Seelios took a deep breath, which only seemed to aggravate the pain. When he reached around with his hand, he found no blood. His ribs, however, felt like they were shattered.

"Is anyone there?" Seelios yelled. His voice echoed through an endless stretch of forest in every direction.

Seelios slowly moved toward a nearby tree and propped himself against the trunk. The task felt like it took an eternity, every small motion resulting in a jolt of pain. His surroundings didn't look familiar and assumed something must have gone wrong with the teleportation totem. He looked down at the artifact still clutched in his hand, lines of bright light traced its edges and yellow runes glowed within the marble gem. It was warm, almost too warm to hold.

Seelios shoved his hand into his tunic and rummaged around until he found the rejuvenation stone. Its runes brimmed with a fiery light, flashing and sparkling as if the sun was trapped within its core. He felt an energy within it unlike anything he'd felt from an artifact before, far greater than what Gregory imbued within it earlier. He looked down at his ring and saw it too shined with runes of radiant brilliance.

Eager to make himself well, Seelios focused on the stone in his hand. His mind connected to the artifact with ease and tapped into the stored mana like a water spicket. His draw from the stone was slow and cautious, letting the warm energy crawl up his arm like a gentle caress. A painful, yet pleasurable, buzz spread through his body as the broken bones in his chest joined back together. The very fibers felt like they were reattaching and settling back into place. Fresh wounds turned to scabs that flaked off as if they'd been there for weeks.

He stood up, glad to move without tormenting his body. He took note that he would need to find a safer way to use the teleportation totem as he pocketed the two runic artifacts.

A rustling noise from the nearby brush made Seelios jump. He crouched behind a tree and strained his ears to the silence of the forest. The snap of a twig echoed through the woods. He slowly stood and scanned the shadows. A familiar pair of ears appeared, followed by a snort he'd heard more times than he could count.

"Acorn!" Seelios shouted.

The horse whipped its head in his direction and looked

at him with a cautious eye. Her muscles twitched, as if prepping to take off at a moment's notice.

Seelios approached the horse with steps so light he could've been walking on a cloud. "Easy, girl. It's just me."

He reached out to touch the brown fur of her nose. She jerked her head away, sending Seelios's heart racing, but she remained standing where she was. He walked beside her and brushed her neck with his hand. Acorn craned around and eyed him for a moment, then lowered her head to chew on a pink flower.

Seelios noticed a familiar leather flask hanging off the side of the saddle. He picked it up and turned it over in his hand. He lifted his eyes and looked around the trees.

"Garrick?" Seelios called out to the woods. Nothing but the rustling of leaves and a peaceful silence sat in place of a reply.

He slipped his foot into one of the stirrups and swung his other leg over the saddle.

Seelios leaned down and patted Acorn's neck. "You had Garrick with you, didn't you? Can you take me to him?"

Acorn lifted her head and turned to eye Seelios again. There had always been an unspoken bond between him and the horse. He could sense the hesitancy, the fear even. Seelios could tell something was wrong, but if Garrick was in trouble he had to go to him.

Seelios sat up straight in the saddle and grabbed the reins. "Come on, girl."

IT WASN'T LONG before Seelios heard the rushing water of the Brascella River. It made perfect sense for Garrick to follow the river. It was one of the few guides that would lead to Paloise, plus it served as a source of water and food.

The trees began to thin, and soft sounds of the river had become a churning roar of rapids. Acorn tossed her head and stopped in her tracks, refusing to go any farther. Seelios felt her tense, and she began backing up. Her head turned to the side as if to go back, but Seelios pulled the reins to turn her forward again.

"What is it, girl?" Seelios whispered down to Acorn.

He slowly sat back up in his saddle and looked ahead. He had a feeling something horrible awaited him, but he had to press on.

Seelios slid off the saddle and stroked Acorn's mane with his hand. "I won't make you go. But please, don't leave me." He looked deep into the horse's eye. Garrick would've said she's just a dumb animal, but to Seelios she was the smartest horse in the land. Acorn nuzzled Seelios's hand, then lowered herself to the ground, folding her legs underneath.

Seelios took a moment to collect himself and prepare for whatever would greet him. He emerged through the trees into a clearing that looked all too familiar. His heart quickened when he took in his surroundings, recognizing the place from his childhood. The artifact had worked after all.

An acrid, rotten stench reached Seelios's nostrils that smelled an order of magnitude worse than the blighted crops in Fembleton. He brought up a sleeve to stifle it, but he would've had to suffocate himself to keep away the odor. He dropped his arm and let his nose brave the journey.

Between the nostalgia and distraction of the smell, Seelios didn't notice the body laying in the sand right away, the surrounding sand stained with blood. He slowly stepped out from the tree line, circling a pile of rocks that had a shiny black goo congealed in its center.

He crept closer and saw curly red hair sprawled across the sand. He sprinted and dropped to his knees beside

Emeline to check her breathing, but could tell from the cold of her skin that she had long passed.

He pulled away the dark stained shirt that was draped over her chest and recoiled at the sight. A sword had been buried in her chest, the hilt encrusted with dried blood.

"Who could've done this to you?" Seelios said with a quiver in his voice. His eyes fell onto a green vest that lay on the ground. Disbelief and horror mixed with a dreaded realization that he tried to force out of his head. He looked back down at the sword and recognized his father's craftsmanship, confirming his terrible suspicion.

Seelios took a moment to whisper a silent apology, then wrapped a hand around the sword's hilt, slid the blade out, and let it fall to the ground beside her. The metal was streaked with blood from base to tip.

Seelios lifted his eyes from Emeline's body, searched the clearing, and discovered the source of the rotten smell. In a part of the forest farthest from the river, the trees sagged in lifeless brown posture, shrinking away from a gaping hole that tunneled deep into the woods.

Black, wrinkled leaves blanketed the ground beneath pale trees with branches that twisted into the air, as if they cried out in pain in their final moments. Grass, bushes, and other vegetation had withered away into a carpet of blighted wilt that lined the floor of the tunnel leading into the shadows.

Something Seelios wasn't prepared to face awaited him within. He thought back to the last time he saw Garrick in the tavern, where he first mentioned his nightmares. If only he had done more to help his friend then. If only he had listened. It might have been too late to do anything, but Seelios had to try.

Even with the bright and sunny sky shining through the

withered limbs, he felt like he was enveloped in darkness as he stepped through the tunnel. The haunting sight of so much death was unlike anything he'd ever experienced.

SEELIOS HAD BEEN WALKING for half an hour when he spotted someone standing in shadows, deep within the dead forest. The brawny, shirtless figure faced away, unmoving.

An overwhelming stench of rot and decay forced Seelios to gag several times, threatening to empty the contents of his stomach onto the black forest floor. This figure seemed to be the source of it all, spreading an aura of death.

Seelios kept his eyes fixed on the figure's back as he approached. He didn't bother keeping his footsteps silent as the dead leaves and branches crunched underfoot like a crisp layer of snow.

"I'm here, Garrick," Seelios said in as soothing a voice as he could muster.

The figure slowly lifted his head, but Seelios still couldn't see his face.

"I found Acorn." Seelios took a step forward. "And Emeline."

No response came.

"Did you do that to her?" Seelios asked.

Seelios took another step, almost within reach of his friend. "I didn't listen to you earlier, about your nightmares. But I see what it's doing to you. Come with me to Paloise. They can help you."

The figure whirled around so fast that Seelios jumped back. Garrick's face was contorted with rage. His eyes were black as midnight. He had the look of someone whose humanity had long abandoned him. Another wave of stench came, causing Seelios's stomach to lurch once again.

"It's too late for me," Garrick said. His eyes twitched as he spoke.

The anger in his face had a momentary lapse as the darkness seemed to subside. His black eyes turned to sadness as he looked at Seelios. He had the look of a man with deep regret, giving in to something he tried to escape, but knew he couldn't.

"I killed her. The only person left whom I truly loved. And I'll kill you if you don't leave," Garrick said, his voice raspy and unrecognizable.

"No, it's not too late. I can help you," Seelios said. He took another step and reached out.

Garrick swatted Seelios's arm away with a force that nearly ripped his shoulder from its socket.

"Be gone!" Garrick yelled. The noise thundered in Seelios's ears and reached into the depths of his soul. The voice that spoke wasn't his friend's, but someone else.

Garrick turned and sprinted into the trees. Green leaves and branches shrunk and curled away as he sped through the forest.

Seelios called out, but Garrick was gone.

13

Seelios clutched at his throbbing arm where Garrick struck him. He'd considered using the rejuvenation stone again, but thought it best to conserve the mana. The pain would pass on its own.

Seelios followed the trail of rotten vegetation back to the clearing. He stood there for the span of several minutes, looking at Emeline lying in the sand. The surrounding trees and setting sun made the area quite beautiful. It was as fitting a place as any for Emeline to be buried.

The soft earth near the river was easy to dig with hands. Seelios scooped out a shallow grave until he reached the harder, colder earth underneath that barely gave way against his fingernails. He walked over to Emeline, picked up the sword that lay beside her, and began to use it to pry chunks of the ground. He scooped out the walls until it was as even as he could manage.

Satisfied, he soaked the green vest in the river and used it to wipe the dried blood from Emeline's face and clean the bloodstains on her dress as best as he could. He wasn't strong enough to carry her, so he laid her on Garrick's tunic and slid her across the sand. Pulling her by the feet, he slowly dragged her into the bottom of her grave.

With Emeline's arms folded across her chest, he placed a single wildflower in her grasp and stepped out to look at her one last time. Her face looked calm and relaxed, as if she knew nothing but joy in her life. She looked beautiful, even in death.

Seelios bowed his head and closed his eyes. "You were the kindest person I ever knew. May the gods watch over you."

Filling the grave with dirt was a much easier process than digging, and there was a certain satisfaction when he rounded out the top of the grave with the last bit of earth. He placed another bouquet of flowers at the peak of the mound. Seelios looked at the sword laying nearby, its metal glinting in the light between the wet clumps of dirt caked to the blade. He picked it up and looked over the blood stains. The very symbol of the horror that transpired, the loss of an innocent life to a weapon that should've been used to protect her. He plunged the blade into the head of the mound to serve as a headstone, letting it be known to any god or mortal what happened in that clearing.

The sun was getting close to the distant horizon over the river, and in a few hours would settle into night. If Seelios left right away he could put some miles between himself and this sad place while there was still light. He made his way back through the woods until he came to the spot where Acorn was supposed to wait for him, but she was nowhere to be found.

"Acorn!" Seelios shouted. He darted his eyes all around and saw the silhouette of Acorn's ears against the reflecting sun on the water.

Acorn lowered her head to take a drink and continued to

stare across the river. She turned her head to eye Seelios for a moment when he approached, then returned to the water.

"Here you are," Seelios said as he placed a hand on her neck, rubbing it gently. "It's time to leave, girl."

Seelios looked up at the sky, fast approaching twilight. They wouldn't have much time on the road, but he was eager to get to Paloise as soon as possible.

"Come on, let's cover a little ground." Seelios tugged at Acorn's reins, but she was unyielding to his pull.

Acorn snorted at Seelios and lowered herself to the ground, tucking her legs underneath. He was starting to get to know the stubborn side of his horse.

Seelios gave a sigh. "I suppose we've both had enough of today. We'll make camp here then."

He gathered kindling from branches strewn across the forest floor and built a fire on a bare patch of ground between two gnarled trees. Acorn walked over and sprawled out on her side by the comforting flames. Seelios didn't realize how exhausted he was until he scooted over and leaned against her soft fur, nodding off to sleep.

The soft chirping of morning birds woke Seelios. When he opened his eyes, he saw the faintest beginning of a new day's light stretch across the sky. The pressure from his bladder roused him to his feet, and he started walking deeper into the forest to relieve himself. Acorn lifted her head as he stepped through the brush.

"I'll be back," Seelios whispered to the horse.

Not wanting to risk getting lost in the dark, he didn't travel too far. He turned and squinted through the branches, making sure he could see the path that would lead him back to the camp site.

He reached down to undo his belt, but stopped when he heard something moving in the trees. He looked up and saw a pair of glowing green eyes staring at him from the foliage. At first, Seelios thought it was animal hiding within the thick of the leaves, but realized as the thing moved that it was made of the forest itself. It stepped out and had the appearance of large stag, yet instead of flesh and fur it was made of stone and moss. Great winding antlers of gnarled wood twisted out from its skull of granite. A great mane of swaying willow hung down the sides of its head and down its neck. Its legs were thick trunks of wood with vines sinewing up and burrowing into its body.

Sensing it was a creature of the earth, Seelios tried taking a step back, but his feet pulled against something that trapped them to the ground. Panic swelled in his chest, and he tried grabbing at nearby branches to pull himself out of what he thought to be a patch of quicksand. Plates of rock slid up his legs and gathered around his torso. His hands touched the hard edges of jagged stone and minerals that twisted over his shoulders and crawled down the length of his arms. His arms and body became so weighed down that the only thing he could move was his head. Even if he was stronger, there was little he could've done to break free.

A deep chuckle echoed through the trees. "You make your great escape only to flee to a forest? You're nothing but a fool without that old man."

Wispy green light engulfed the earthen stag as it rose up on two legs. Antlers shrank back into dark hair and the rocky exterior of the earth creature turned to shimmering armor.

The green light faded and the God of Earth stood, smiling through his thick black beard. "This is my domain," he said as he struck his armored chest with a fist, sending his green cape billowing out to the side in regal grace.

The god thrust his hand through the stone encasing Seelios's chest and rummaged around his tunic, grabbing the teleportation totem. He pulled it out, and the rock slid back into place. Even if Seelios wasn't trapped, he would've been paralyzed with fear.

Seelios calmed his nerves as best as he could. "Why? Why kill us? Gameus, you're supposed to protect us."

The god narrowed his glowing green eyes. "You dare address me as anything other than Lord of the Earth? Your arrogance is astounding."

The rock tightened around Seelios. He winced from the pain, but pushed it aside and continued. "What do you gain from all this? We've done nothing to threaten you."

Gameus chuckled. "Such is the mind of a naive child. I've lived for eons. Humans are mere insects in the cycle of all things of this world and the next. If you think humans threaten me, you're even more idiotic than I thought. A war is coming with an outcome at stake far greater than any amount of human life. Your father's involvement is paramount, and I kill those who stand in my way of finding him."

"What is it you want with my father?" Seelios asked.

Gameus scoffed. "It matters not. You were going to be my means of getting him, but after seeing what you're capable of, I've decided to turn my attention to you."

Seelios swallowed nervously. "And so now you'll kill me?"

The God of Earth sneered. "I want to, boy. The frustration of your father escaping my grasp and you eluding me twice now is enough to make me smite you across this forest floor."

Gameus walked up to Seelios and narrowed his eyes, staring deep into his soul. "But your recent escape has shown me something. What you did in Alnerwick, drawing mana from the sun, it's unheard of for a mortal. There's a part of you that's yet to be fully awakened. You have a place in this war, and far be it for me to stand in the way of that . . . for now."

While the god spoke, Seelios struggled against the earthly restraints. The rock was so tight on his arms that he couldn't even slide an inch and only succeeded in scuffing his skin. He needed a way to escape. His eyes fell to the teleportation totem in the god's hand.

Gameus held the artifact up. "Indeed, it came so easily to you. At least, more easily than anyone else in your circumstances. It's a pity you're so reliant on it. Anyone with half a mind and your talents would use their mana to surge their strength and break free from my hold." The god gave a mocking chuckle. "Still, you are impressive. I've heard teleportation isn't an easy feat."

Seelios wanted to believe the god had good intentions, but he killed so many. He couldn't trust that the god actually wanted him to live. Not with Seelios being held prisoner.

The ring on Seelios's finger grew warm. He had a burning sensation to use it, but even if he activated it he couldn't bring his hand up to peer through it.

The god turned away from Seelios and walked through the trees. The branches and leaves moved like a parting sea. The ground swelled as roots snapped and trees groaned, giving away to the shifting earth. A throne of shimmering rock broke through the dirt and lifted to nearly the height of Seelios. The God of Earth sat himself down with a swish of his cape, facing Seelios again.

"You want to use it, don't you?" the god said, nodding toward the ring on Seelios's hand.

Seelios said nothing, feeling as if he was being toyed with.

The God of Earth leaned forward in his seat and smiled. "My puppets told me of your use of the thing." He gave another chuckle. "You use it like a child just learning the ways of the world, no understanding of its full purpose."

The god leaned back in his chair and rested his head on his hand, extending a finger along his cheek.

"I'll make a bargain with you. I'll release you if you can show me that you can use the ring without lifting it to your eye. If not, I may just leave you here forever."

Seelios's eyes flickered in distress. The thought of being imprisoned in the middle of the woods for eternity sounded like a nightmare. Even if someone found him, there'd be no way to get him out.

He reined in his panic and tried to focus. If he heard the God of Earth right, there was a way to use the ring without actually having to take it off. Seelios felt the runic artifact's pulse around his finger, as if it were eager to rise to the challenge. The last two artifacts he was able to activate resulted from near-death experiences, but he had no plan to do that again. His only chance of success with the ring was to shut out everything around him and clear his mind.

Seelios closed his eyes and steadied his breathing. He heard nothing around him except the soft sounds of the forest. He felt his heart slow to the calming beat of the ring's mana. He began to understand, like a sudden remembrance of a memory from a dream. The Alnerwick sun had given him a gift of knowledge he didn't truly discern until now. The artifact wasn't a tool; it was a reminder. It contained a memory of something that was already embedded within

Seelios. With this, he used the familiar feeling of the ring as a guiding compass and searched his own self.

It didn't take long for him to find the familiar sensation of the ring's power within himself. It was like rediscovering an emotion that had been long forgotten, much like how a smell could unlock a flood of latent memories.

Inexplicable feelings of nostalgia came surging into his mind, even though he had no memory of doing this before. The connection he'd felt in the past when using the truth ring suddenly filled his whole body, enveloping him in a power that was previously limited to just the artifact. It surged through him, free and unrestrained.

"Yes," the God of Earth whispered.

Seelios slowly opened his eyes to a world he had only seen through a tiny stone circle before. He could see everything around him with a deeper understanding of the life within. Each of the trees had flowing streams of light that ran through their trunks and fanned out among branches and leaves like fluorescent spiderwebs. He scanned his surroundings before he settled on the brimming silhouette of the God of Earth.

Seelios was met with shock. He'd expected Gameus's aura to be black as night, but instead the god was almost pure white except for a jagged, electric mass of yellow and black in his heart. Most auras he'd witnessed were gray and muddled, confused and full of doubt. But this one had such a sharp, colliding contrast. There was good in the god, yet something evil within his heart. He'd seen similar before, but only within people full of terror. Whatever Gameus feared, it looked to be driven by the growing blackness.

Seelios looked at Gameus for a moment, taking in the nakedness of his soul. "You're afraid of something, aren't you?"

Gameus's face transitioned from one of mild awe to annoyance and rage. "You mean to tell me that with this kind of power, you choose to cower while those around you suffer and die?" The god's voice boomed with a ferocity that shook surrounding branches and leaves, releasing flocks of birds into the sky.

Seelios regarded the god in stunned silence. The outburst broke Seelios's concentration and his vision of flowing light melted away into the muted colors of mortal eyes.

The god stood from his throne and stepped forward, inches from Seelios's face. "You're pathetic. You disgrace all that the God of Light represents."

The stone surrounding Seelios cracked and shattered, falling to the ground in a pile of dusty rubble. Gameus shoved the teleportation totem into Seelios's chest so hard it knocked the wind from him. Seelios stumbled backward, nearly tripping over the rock remains. He looked down at the artifact, his chest still aching.

"If you follow the river you'll reach Paloise in four days, even with that small horse of yours. There you can continue to hide while the world around you is devoured." Gameus held a smoldering gaze on Seelios, then turned, and walked deeper into the forest. He stopped and said over his shoulder, "The disciple you were traveling with is still held captive by my pets in Alnerwick. He will die soon."

The earth began to rumble as the ground split apart beneath the god. Green light shone up from the fissure, and he disappeared between the cracks.

14

S eelios stood in the middle of the forest, stunned by the words of Gameus. While it was true Seelios had obvious power, it still didn't feel like he'd be able to make a difference. Even if he managed to teleport back to Alnerwick, he had no idea how he would defeat the rock golem, a creature of stone impervious to blades. Anything short of a heavy siege weapon would be useless.

The morning sun began to peer through overhead branches, bringing the forest to life around Seelios. Aside from the scattering of broken rocks, there was hardly a sign a threatening god had been there. The trees had returned to their normal positions, with a more vibrant green to them than before. Flowers bloomed all around, even the moss seemed to be sprouting with more life.

The serenity of the forest was something he'd been missing since he left Fembleton. Seelios hadn't known peace since Gameus's first attack, constantly in fear of danger. But now that safety was only four days away, Seelios couldn't help but think that maybe the God of Earth was right.

Maybe it wasn't the right time to be safe, to seek shelter and hide.

Seelios made his way back to his camp where Acorn stood, patiently waiting for him.

"I'm sorry, girl," he said as he brushed her mane. "But I have to go, and you can't come with me."

She nuzzled his arm and tugged at his sleeve with her mouth.

"Paloise isn't far from here. Follow the river, don't stop for anything," Seelios said. "Go. Sprint if you must. Just get there as safely as you can."

He pushed her head aside and backed away, but she trotted after him. She nuzzled his hand, pushing her nose underneath his palm.

"Acorn," Seelios whispered as he wrapped his arms around her neck in an embrace.

He smelled the musty scent of her sweat, causing memories of Fembleton to come flooding back. He remembered the days of playing in Garrick's fields and browsing through books of stories and legends in his library. Such simple times, where the greatest concern was whether or not they'd be caught sneaking around the forge while Ricker was out. Their greatest find was discovering Ricker's secret cache of his finest weapons.

Seelios's eyes went wide with realization.

He let go of Acorn and stepped away again, fiddling through his pockets, and pulled out the teleportation totem. He stared at it in his hand, still brimming with mana.

He looked up at Acorn and said, "Wish me luck."

Seelios closed his eyes and focused on the one place he knew better than anything else in his life: home.

SEELIOS ALMOST LANDED on his feet when he saw the ground materialize beneath him. Despite his anticipation, the cobbled road rushed up at him with surprising speed and he hit it harder than he would've liked. The shock of the landing made his teeth hurt. He tried to tuck into a roll but only managed to flop to the ground on his back. It was still a significant improvement over his last teleportation attempt, managing to at least stay conscious.

Bright light slowly faded and Seelios could begin to make out the shapes of buildings. Blurry lines sharpened and the familiar landscape of the market square took form. But it wasn't the happy place he once knew. Broken pieces of rock and debris were scattered everywhere. What once had been a bustling place of commerce was littered with houses and shops torn asunder. There were craters from where Gameus had unleashed a hail of boulders. He wondered where the golems had gone.

Anger welled up within Seelios. Gameus called him a coward for not acting when the attack happened, but it was Gameus himself who should not have attacked in the first place. Just like how Gameus should not be holding a Disciple of Light hostage. Seelios wished he'd found the courage to say all this to the god while they were in the forest, but it didn't matter, his actions would speak louder.

He picked himself up and made his way through the ruins, toward the forge by the river. With most of the buildings razed to the ground, Seelios could see the Southern Mountains spanning in the distance beyond the sparkling water of Fembleton's lake. His father was somewhere out there. Seelios only hoped that he was safe, wherever he might be.

Seelios squeezed between the cobbler's shop and a large piece of the tailor's broken wall and saw the half standing forge. There was a gaping hole where the entire right side of the building should've been, as if a giant kicked it in and collapsed much of the structure in on itself.

The inside of the forge was just as much a mess as the outside. The stone brick that made up the wall lay in heaps on the floor. Many of the tools and various items were missing from shelves and racks, likely buried under rubble or tangled with the wood debris of splintered scaffolding and broken furniture.

Seelios stepped on the lip of the crumbling wall and placed a light foot on top of a sturdy pile of rubble. He carefully made his way down into the depths of the ruined forge by easing down their collapsed thatched roofing, trying his best not to turn an ankle on the loose debris. He climbed over the dust covered anvil and stepped around a fallen shelf of tools. The corner where the weapon's cache lay had a small heap of stone bricks crumbled in front. His whole body strained as he gripped the stones with both hands and hefted them aside, surprised that he found the strength. They clacked and rolled, kicking dust back up into the air that sent him into the occasional coughing fit. When he was finished, his hands felt raw and his back stiff. Sweat covered his whole body and he felt soreness seizing his muscles.

The loose stones next to the heavy shelf came up with ease and revealed the tracks in the floor. Seelios took a moment to catch his breath before gripping the massive piece of furniture. This time he didn't have Garrick to help him. He braced his foot against the wall and pushed with all his might. The shelf screeched with an ear piercing pitch as the metal slid through unoiled ruts in the ground.

Whether Seelios's pulse was pounding from the physical labor or sheer adrenaline, he didn't know. But when he looked into the darkness of the hidden room and saw glittering metal, he felt as if his heart were going to leap out of his chest. The cache was exactly how he'd remembered it in his youth. It was built like a small closet with shelves lining the sides and a wooden rack in the back. They held stacks of coins and a small box with various scrolls, notes, and maps. Seelios would've loved to browse his father's private collection, but the lack of time and guilt of invading privacy made him decide against it.

He turned his eyes to the weapons rack in the back. The selection was much smaller than he recalled, expecting to see at least a couple swords and some pieces to a suit of armor. The only item that remained was a single spear standing upright in the middle: the spear he came for.

Seelios reached in and lifted the weapon with a single hand, surprised at its lightness. He carried it out and stepped into the light. Curling engravings swirled up the shining metal of the shaft with such beautiful elegance that, despite his father's remarkable craftsmanship, made Seelios question if an even greater smith had forged it. The head of the spear rippled with waves of bronze and gold, the colored pattern of a metal so sharp that it could pierce a rock golem.

SEELIOS MADE his careful trek out of the crumbling forge and stepped onto the dirt road. He hefted the spear in his hand, testing its balance in his palm. He switched from one arm to the other, feeling which he was more comfortable with. With a two handed grip he spread his stance, leaned forward, and stabbed at the air. Halfway through the motion his body went electric with pain and his limbs went limp. He barely clung to the spear as the tip dropped to the ground. The soreness had taken its toll and his back didn't even retain the flexibility to perform a simple spear jab. He let the spear fall with a thud and massaged his muscles. The tenderness was so great he could barely stand the prodding of his own fingers. He was in no shape to fight off any enchanted rock creatures.

Seelios gave a sigh as he pulled out the rejuvenation stone and looked at its shimmering yellow runes. "I haven't even tried to fight yet and I already need to use this."

Strength returned to his muscles and his back relaxed as the mana left the stone and spread through his body. The runes' shimmer lost a bit of their luster, but they still remained illuminated. Seelios would need to be smart about his use of the artifacts if he was going to survive his rescue mission.

He picked the spear up and tried a few more practice maneuvers. His jabs, recovers, and parries came surprisingly natural to him once he'd given his muscles the needed energy.

Satisfied with his performance, he pulled the teleportation totem and rejuvenation stone out of his pockets and tucked them into his tunic. He gave his torso a few turns and felt the runic artifacts shift around against his rib cage. He thought for a moment, then ran back into the forge. He dug through some of the debris near the door and uncovered an old traveler's cloak that his father kept on a peg by the entrance. He tore a long shred of cloth from it and wrapped it around his mid-section several times, cinching the artifacts tight to his body.

He stepped back outside and held the spear upright. There was no more time to waste, Seelios needed to go. He'd thought being a hero would be fun and exhilarating, but the only thing he felt was fear. He closed his eyes, took a deep breath, and felt the light envelop him as his feet left the ground.

15

When Seelios performed his teleportation to Alnerwick, he focused on the outer farm with all of his mental might. If he managed to materialize his body on the town's perimeter, he could sneak into the square unnoticed, free Gregory, and flee with minimal conflict. Whether it was his nerves or novice experience with teleportation totem, his plan did not go as expected.

The light faded as Seelios's feet gracefully touched down onto hard earth. He was so excited with his landing that he barely noticed Gregory laying in front of him on the remains of a wooden deck. Seelios blinked down at the disciple who was covered in dirt, blood seeping from his mouth. Gregory's eyes slowly opened and went wide as they followed the motion of something behind Seelios.

Terror and realization dawned on Seelios and he dove aside in a desperate move to get out of harm's way. A thunderous crash shook the ground as he slid across the ground. Dirt and rock peppered his back as debris rained all around him.

He picked himself up and scrambled to grab his spear. He spun and readied the shining weapon with both hands. A rock golem lifted its massive, rune-covered fist out of a crater where Seelios had been moments before, and leered in his direction. The force of the golem's impact shook the remains of a nearby building to the ground, causing a wall to fall down in a tumble of stone bricks.

The rest of Alnerwick looked to be demolished just like Fembleton. The inn where Seelios and Gregory had stayed looked as if a massive tree fell atop it, pulverizing wood and stone into a sea of rubble. Surrounding buildings were seemingly annihilated in similar fashion, to the point where most of them were unrecognizable. The golem must've been hard at work while Seelios was away, leveling everything within sight.

Lurking about the ruins of buildings were several clay men of poor, yet disturbing, imitation to Seelios, Gregory, and other people he didn't recognize. Their faces were warped and grotesque, giving haunting visions of disfigurement. Others had near nothing on their face, staring out with a pair of eyes on a blank oval of clay. They remained in the distance behind fallen walls, watching.

"Why are you here?" Gregory said. The sound of his voice seemed to strain for a yell, but only managed out a raspy whisper. "I told you to run."

The golem stomped toward Seelios with green, glowing eyes that stared at him with menace.

"I came to rescue you." Seelios backed away as he kept his eyes fixed on the hulking rock monster. The enormous thing had arms that far out-ranged his spear. He questioned whether this was a rescue mission or a suicide.

He planted his feet and forced himself to remember what he was there for. He was done being the victim, a spectator to destruction. All along he had the ability to do something but was too afraid to do it. He looked down at the head of the spear and remembered what his father said about orichalcum. If it was truly the metal of the gods, the golem wouldn't stand a chance.

The distance between Seelios and the golem was closed in three strides of the towering giant. Seelios crouched down like a coiled viper, spear leveled at the wide stone torso. The golem took another step and lifted its arm up to reveal a mile-wide opening. Seelios saw the opportunity and lunged forward. The golem brought its arm down so fast it was nearly a blur. It's palm collided into Seelios with a force that made his jaw go numb.

He saw sky and earth as he cartwheeled through the air. He landed on hard dirt, rolling for several feet before skidding to a stop, face down. Stars danced around his eyes and he tasted blood in his mouth. He tried to use the rejuvenation stone tucked into his tunic, but his mind couldn't latch onto it. He reached to his chest and the motion sent searing pain across his shoulder that radiated up his neck. He used the fingers of his other hand to grope across his chest and felt nothing but the teleportation totem. When he lifted his head he saw the rejuvenation stone glimmering in the dust a few feet away.

Seelios tried to pull a leg underneath of him but was met with a pain so great it nearly made him vomit. He felt as if there wasn't a single bone in his body that was whole. Even with his greatest summoning of will power, Seelios was only able to move a couple inches before a crushing weight pinned his legs to the ground. Seelios screamed as all feeling left the lower half of his body. His body grew weaker by the moment and felt death was nearly upon him.

He craned his neck to see the golem towering over him,

driving its foot into the ground where Seelios's legs were. Even if he managed to grab hold of the rejuvenation stone, he would still need to get out from underneath the golem's weight. He wondered if the runic artifact would even be able to heal all of the injuries his body sustained.

The howl of a battle cry rang out and Walter the innkeep came charging from a ruined shop, brandishing a large wood axe. He swung with two hands and landed a blow against the back of the golem's leg with a clang. Walter brought up the head of the axe and inspected it with a face of disbelief. A large chunk of metal was missing while the golem's leg yielded barely a scratch.

The golem reared its head around and looked at Walter, still keeping its foot on Seelios. Taking advantage of the opportunity, Seelios writhed and twisted under the stony foot, multiplying the pain of his broken bones. Despite his best efforts, he wasn't able to budge. In his movements, he felt the jab of the teleportation totem in his chest. The artifact responded with a glowing warmth that emitted light from inside his tunic.

Seelios didn't have time to concentrate, he just felt the connection with the artifact come as quick as a natural reaction. A flash erupted around him and he found himself sprawled out on the dirt once more, but the pressure from the golem's foot gone. The rejuvenation stone glimmered right beside his face. He realized he'd teleported only a foot, maybe not even, but it was enough to make a world of difference. Straining his barely functioning joints, Seelios rotated his body until his arm flopped across the dirt. As soon as his fingertips made contact he put the runic artifact to use. Bones reconnected and muscles reattached as the warmth flowed once again, relieving searing pain and restoring vigor.

Seelios stood on his feet with renewed courage, but his heart sank when he looked at his hand. The glowing runes on the rejuvenation stone had faded, making it look like an ordinary river stone once again. Cracks appeared and spread over its surface. It had become completely devoid of the thriving mana once within in it.

Seelios looked up at the golem, which fixed its attention back onto him after Walter had ducked back into a maze of rubble. Another hit from the monster and Seelios would have no way to recover. He needed to find a way to end the fight, fast.

He looked down at his empty hands and realized he'd lost his spear. He jerked his head left and right, searching the area when a twinkle of light caught Seelios's attention. The shaft of the orichalcum spear protruded out of the side of a shop's wall. He sprinted for it and the golem stomped after him, sending shock waves through the ground.

A pile of rubble exploded from the swooping arm of the golem and blasted Seelios with rocks and chunks of splintered wood. He shielded his face and body with his arms as he continued to run. He reached the spear and felt his mind slip into a familiar focus. The ring on his hand grew hot and his vision changed, showing flowing lines of mana as they coursed through the buildings and landscape around him. He looked at the spear and could see a bright concentration of light running through the core of the shaft, all the way to the flattened head of the spear blade. It looked like a dazzling star, molded into a tool for destruction. He grabbed the spear and pulled. The wall crumbled away from the shining weapon as it slipped out with ease.

Seelios spun on the golem thundering toward him. When his eyes fell upon the animated rock, seeing with the power of the truth ring, he witnessed it in its purest form.

Sparkling streams of mana bound the boulders at various joints, linking them together. Green light fanned out from a central point in its chest, where its concentration was the greatest.

Seelios jumped backward, just in time to dodge a fist that slammed into the ground. A cloud of dust billowed up and he could see the skeletal form of the golem, mana flowing like blood through transparent limbs. He saw the arm raise up again to strike, the surges of mana displaying its every movement and revealing the secrets of its actions.

Using his newfound perception, Seelios realized that his attempts to fight the golem head-on were futile. No matter when he attacked, the golem's speed and range far outpaced anything that Seelios could respond with. Still, something inside him told him to act, despite the disadvantage.

Seelios lunged forward, preparing for the impact of the golem's hand. Another surge of razor-sharp focus overtook him and light flashed from the teleportation totem. The glowing chest of the golem was suddenly so close that he could've reached out and touched it. He found himself sailing forward in mid-air, inside the elbow of the golem's outstretched arm.

Using his momentum, Seelios plunged the spear into the core of green mana. The orichalcum slipped through the rock like a toothpick piercing a soft loaf of bread. He crashed into the golem, then fell to the ground between its feet. He shook the daze from the landing and scrambled away.

The light of the golem's eyes flashed a bright green, then faded to darkness. Strands of light that made up its glowing skeleton shrank until they'd become razor thin lines. It swayed for a moment, the spear shaft sticking out of its chest, then crashed to the ground. The strand of mana connecting its head to the body broke with a sputter of green light, and it rolled away until it rested beside the remains of a house. The remaining lines of green light faded and the limbs dropped to the ground with deep thuds, once again ordinary stones.

Seelios sat on the ground, staring at the pile of inanimate stones that had been responsible for so much destruction. His gaze lingered for a long moment, taking in what he thought to be impossible. He had won. He felled the giant and saved the town, at least what was left of it.

Seelios stood and dusted himself off. When he looked up, he saw the surrounding clay men staring at him from behind half-standing walls. He climbed atop the chest of the rock golem and pulled the spear. He turned to the clay men and readied himself to fight, but they remained. He wondered if they were waiting for reinforcements, or even the God of Earth himself. Or maybe they were just struck with awe.

The clay men slowly began to shrink away. They turned their backs and fled to the surrounding trees in their awkward gaits. Seelios watched the essence of their mana crumble and sink into the ground as they retreated into the earth to join their master.

Seelios realized that he'd never truly taken a long look at the world with the power of the truth ring. He swept his gaze over the surrounding landscape, seeing the flowing life of trees and animals far in the distance that would otherwise be blocked from sight. Jutting out of the horizon was a tower gleaming with light, stretching up high into the sky.

A single cry of victory rang out from behind a wall, jostling Seelios out of his focused gaze. The tower of light faded into blue of the sky as his vision reverted back to normal. More shouts followed as villagers poured out from their hiding places. Some mourned over the destruction of their homes while others collapsed in tears, thankful to still be alive. Reunited families hugged each other as if they'd never let go again. Seelios watched the villagers, smiling at the sight of them happy to be with each other. He realized then that he found more purpose in saving those people than anything else he'd done in his life.

A crowd gathered in front of the shop with the sagging blue awning. Seelios jogged over and the crowd split, revealing Gregory laying where he'd been before. The disciple formed a smile when their eyes met.

"You've done it," he whispered.

Villagers looked at Seelios with smiles, nodding in agreement.

"Who are you, boy, and where do you come from?" a man's voice asked. Walter, the innkeeper, stepped out from the crowd.

"My name is Seelios. I'm from a small village in the foothills of the Southern Mountains."

"Seelios. We will remember that name for the rest of our lives. Thank you for saving us." Walter bowed his head. The other villagers did the same.

"What do we do now?" another voice asked from the crowd.

"Our homes are destroyed, there's nothing left," someone else said.

Murmurs erupted from the crowd as the villagers exchanged worried looks and shared concerns.

"Silence," Walter said. "Let the young man speak."

The crowd grew quiet and all eyes fell back on Seelios. He looked around at the expectant faces. Not sure what to say, he looked down at Gregory.

"These people are your responsibility now, Seelios," the

disciple said. He winced as he spoke, as if the action pained him. If only the rejuvenation stone were still intact.

Seelios looked back at the faces of the villagers. There were men and women, even children, who had faces of fear and despair. He knew how they felt, suddenly uprooted from their homes, losing all sense of security. Gregory was right, these people were terrified that something like this might happen to them again. Without Seelios's intervention, they probably wouldn't have survived.

Seelios looked down at Gregory. "I need to take this man to Paloise. Come with us. My home too was destroyed by the God of Earth and I am lost, just like you, but we can find another home together."

Murmurs broke out again as people nodded their heads in agreement. After experiencing the devastation of a golem, none of them were eager to stay. The crowd slowly dispersed as people ran off to ready wagons and pack supplies.

PEOPLE BEGAN to gather at the village square, bringing all their belongings in travel sacks and pack horses. Some brought what was left of their livestock while others stood empty-handed. Those who lost everything were taken in by others who had some left to give, offering clothes and food. Wagons were shared and carefully packed to the brim so that everyone could take their essentials.

Seelios and a few other men gently lifted Gregory into the back of a covered wagon with the other injured. The town physician crouched, tending to the wounds of those that needed it most.

"Please, take care of him," Seelios said as he backed away from the wagon.

The healer looked up at him through thick glasses. "Perhaps you can show me how to use that stone of yours?"

Seelios reached into his pocket and pulled out the rejuvenation stone. He felt nothing as he held it in his palm, its surface scarred with a web of cracks.

"I wish I could," Seelios said.

Villagers milled about, sorting through the rubble and gathering the last bits of their belongings. It wasn't long before all of the horses were packed to their limit. The wagon loads were bulging out the sides.

Seelios was about to help a woman when he felt a tug on his tunic from behind. He turned and saw the smiling face of a young boy looking up at him, no more than four or five years old. He had dark brown eyes and a thick head of shaggy black hair.

"You're really strong, aren't you?" the boy said.

"I . . . well, no not particularly," Seelios said with a smile.

The boy swung his arms from side to side, looking down at the ground. "But that monster was really scary and you killed it."

Walter walked up beside them. "Come now, you know better than to bother people who are busy." He put a hand on the boy's head and tousled his hair. The innkeeper turned and smiled at Seelios. "Sorry about that, he's a curious one. This is my son, Elrick." He looked down at the little boy. "You need to go be with your mother. Go on, say goodbye to Seelios."

The boy looked down and started kicking the dirt. "Goodbye Mr. Seelios. Sorry to bother you."

Seelios chuckled. "It's alright, Elrick."

They both watched the boy scurry off to a blonde woman in a dark blue dress, standing near one of the wagons. She smiled as he ran up to her, scooping him up in her arms and smothering him with kisses. Seelios and Walter laughed together as Elrick squirmed and turned his face away in revulsion. Such sweet moments reminded Seelios of his own childhood, except he never did have a mother to shower him with affection.

Walter turned to face Seelios. "What you did for us, returning here and killing that creature, it was the greatest feat of bravery I'd ever seen." He frowned as he looked around. "The others, they might look like they're fine, but I know these people, they're terrified. Not only of another attack, but to leave this place. Most have known no other land except what you see before you, including myself." He placed a hand on Seelios's shoulder and smiled. "But you've given us the courage we need. That's why we want you to lead us."

Walter gestured toward an open horse-drawn wagon at the head of the caravan that had formed. The people of Alnerwick stood around it, waiting for Seelios to take his seat as their guide.

16

I t was common knowledge that the surest path to Paloise was to follow the Brascella River, but its wide turns and bends around the landscape made for a lengthy journey. The better way was to take a straight route, but no one was well traveled enough to know the way. The Trade Road was another known route to take, but Alnerwick was far from the beaten path. In order to reach either road or river, they had no choice but to travel through the forest, a thought that worried Seelios.

The wagons lurched forward and the caravan made its first tracks out of Alnerwick. Villagers looked longingly at their homes, some appearing stricken with grief at the thought of leaving. Their aimless journey seemed to make them uneasy, but there was nowhere else to go. Still, Seelios wished that he had a better heading on Paloise than just a plan to follow a long river somewhere in the woods. There must have been a better way.

An answer appeared when the tree line sprung to life with an extravagant blossoming of flowers. Vibrant colors of pink, purple, red, and yellow bloomed between leaves off branches and vines that wound up trunks. The flower petals opened and stretched out, forming an arch that framed an entrance to the forest. It was inviting and beautiful, the complete opposite of the dead tunnel that Garrick had made. Wispy green eyes emerged as the God of Earth stepped out in his earthen stag form and met Seelios's eyes. He felt his heart jump to his throat. Gasps came from the people behind him as the whole caravan halted.

Seelios focused his thoughts on the power of the truth ring and his vision changed. An aura of benevolence swirled around the god and gave no indication of immediate danger. It would appear that the God of Earth came in peace.

"It's alright," Seelios said as he kept his eyes fixed on the stag. It blinked at him, staring back, then swooshed its mossy mane as it turned back to the forest. It took a few steps and looked back, as if waiting for them to follow.

"It's not here to harm us," Seelios said. He lifted his hand from the orichalcum spear resting next to him and picked up the reins.

Walter ran up beside Seelios. "What are you doing? That thing is an avatar of the God of Earth."

"I know," Seelios said.

"He'll see us dead if we go near!" the innkeeper said.

Seelios looked out at the earthen stag in the distance and remembered the respect the god had given Seelios for his demonstration of power. "He's here to guide us."

"It's a trap," a woman yelled out. "He wants to lure us into the forest."

Seelios stood up in the wagon and turned around. "Gameus has brought death and pain to us all, but if he wanted us dead he could've come here and done it himself. I've seen his power." He stepped down from the wagon. "I know this may be hard for you to believe, but he wishes to see us to safety."

The villagers exchanged looks of worry and concern, whispering amongst themselves and shaking their heads.

"That rock creature killed many of our friends and family. Why would the god help us?" a man said from the crowd.

Voices got louder as the crowd grew angry. People began to walk away and retreat back toward the ruins of Alnerwick.

Walter yelled and quieted the crowd.

"The God of Earth didn't change his mind," Seelios said. "He was looking for someone; someone strong. And now that I've destroyed one of his most powerful minions, he believes that person is me."

Whispers spread through the crowd as they grew calmer.

Seelios pointed to the stag. "Come with me and let the God of Earth guide us to Paloise."

As THE CARAVAN moved closer to the forest, the stag turned and walked deeper into the woods. The flowering trees that framed the entrance widened as Seelios approached. As the stag stepped, gentle waves rippled out through the dirt and left a perfectly smooth path better than any man-made road. Seelios looked at the trees and bushes lining the pathway, vibrant with a natural life that made leaves greener and strips of bark richer in color than anything he'd ever seen in the wild. The very presence of the earthen stag seemed to invigorate the environment around it.

"This seems a bit strange, don't you think?" Walter said,

riding on a horse beside Seelios's wagon. "Why would the God of Earth first attack us, then help us?"

Seelios's mind went to the moment when Gameus held him captive in the woods. He thought about what he had witnessed when he used the truth ring. Deep down the God of Earth had good in him, but there was a source of fear guiding his actions. It drove him to do terrible things, but he wouldn't tell why. Perhaps granting Seelios safe passage to Paloise was somehow addressing that which the god feared.

"I don't know," Seelios said. "All I know is he had the chance to kill me, but wished me to live."

Walter nodded as he seemed to lose himself in thought. "Then I hope you don't leave our side."

Seelios smiled. "Don't worry. I plan to see you and the rest of the villagers to safety."

The trees began to thin ahead and Seelios saw the sparkling water of the Brascella River. It's babbling currents were much calmer than the rapids of Emeline's Clearing.

The caravan stopped at the tree line and watched the stag wade into the shallows. Water splashed about its wooden legs and tugged at its mossy mane. At least there was some assurance that they were headed in the right direction. Even if the stag abandoned them, they'd still be able to follow the river to Paloise.

The god raised its head, tilting its wooden antlers back as he pointed his snout to the sky. The green light of his eyes grew in intensity as he seemed to concentrate in some sort of summoning of power. The sands of the river bank shifted and tree roots snapped, giving way to thick green vines that rose out of the ground. They continued to grow, reaching up above the trees, until they towered menacingly in the air. Seelios grabbed his spear and stood in his wagon. Screams came from the caravan and villagers began backing away.

The writhing vines slowly fell away from the trees and stretched across the river. Water splashed as the giant stalks unfurled across the surface like colossal green tongues. The tips of the vines reached the other side of the river and anchored themselves into the ground with an explosion of dirt, pulling themselves taught to form a living bridge.

Seelios eased back down into the seat of the wagon as he watched the stag step onto the vines and walk across. He looked on with hesitation, but realized the others were watching him. No one else would dare cross the bridge if Seelios didn't even have the courage to do so. He took a deep breath and snapped the reins. Seelios's horse seemed surprisingly calm, as if it were a once a week occurrence for the animal. He remembered what Gregory said about horses being creatures of the earth.

The wheels made strange noises as they squeaked over the slippery surface. It was an odd sensation to be suspended over a river, secured by something that had formed only moments prior. Seelios turned his head and saw the rest of the caravan following. Nearly everyone looked terrified and some didn't even set foot onto the vine bridge until they saw others successfully cross.

By the time dusk arrived everyone was eager to make camp. Discussions were happening up and down the caravan about when they should stop, when the stag suddenly halted before them. It turned to face Seelios and the rest of the villagers. Green eyes flashed as the trees around them shrank away like a crowded plaza making way for their king. Groans of shifting wood and snapping of stray branches echoed all around as they intertwined and packed together to form a dense perimeter around the clearing. Brush, weeds, and other plant-life retreated into small fissures in the ground that sealed themselves up to reveal soft, yet firm earth.

The villagers looked around at the clearing with their mouths agape. It was a perfect place to set up their encampment. At the edge where trees and plants packed together, bushes blossomed with ripe and juicy fruits. People rushed to them and eagerly ate the feast offered by the earth. They turned to face the stag while holding up the fruit and shouted their praise, bowing in respect. The green eyes stared back at them.

An offering given by a god must be accepted with utmost gratitude; a cardinal rule that must be respected with sacred reverence. Whether it be out of devotion or fear, it didn't matter, just that the god was acknowledged for its generosity.

Seelios took a large apple that drooped down from a branch. "Thank you, Lord of the Earth," he said in a deep bow. The stag regarded him with unblinking eyes, then turned and strode into the forest. The trees opened before it, then closed as it nestled down into its own grove of foliage that slithered up from the ground and cradled it like newborn chick in a bird's nest.

"WHAT'S THIS SHIT?" an old man said. From across the fire he could be seen scowling down at a handful of berries. He tossed them over his shoulder and looked at the others. "I need meat! I'm not livestock."

Seelios looked at the man in horror, then glanced over at the stag. It remained unmoving.

"Calm yourself, Byram. We must take what the god offers," Walter said.

"I will not calm myself!" Byram stood and glared at

Walter. "I've been riding in that damned wagon all day. All I ask for is for a proper meal." He glanced over at the grove where the stag lay. "That thing leading us, it's not safe." He pointed a finger at Seelios. "You there. Your spear killed that rock giant. I have a mind to believe you could kill that four-legged pile of dirt."

"Kill it?" another man said. "It's the only thing guiding us through this forest!"

Other villagers murmured in agreement. Some frowned, looking as if they weren't sure what to do. People began talking at once, raising their voices over each other. It was beginning to get so loud that Seelios was concerned the stag would awake.

"Quiet you fools," Walter said as he stood from his seat on a log. He scowled at everyone gathered around the campfire like they were children. "Malicious or not, we best not wake that thing in the middle of the night. Keep your voices down."

"I still have faith in the stag," Seelios said. "You all have every reason not to, as do I, yet here we are. We've come all this way and should see it through to the end."

The murmurs and lack of outward agreement made Seelios suspect that not everyone shared his sentiments. The God of Earth had, after all, destroyed their entire home town and killed many of their loved ones. To not trust the stag would be understandable, but Seelios hoped their hearts wouldn't lead them astray. Or maybe they were right. Maybe Gameus did have something bad in store for them. Still, the god only seemed to have one thing on his mind when he spoke to Seelios, and that was the approaching war. Seelios had been pawing at the chance to share this piece of information with someone, but was hesitant because of the questions he knew would follow.

Who was the war going to be between? When was the war going to happen? How does the God of Earth know about this?

Conversations continued, but no one else found the courage to appeal to the group. Seelios caught glimpses of Byram glaring at him through the flames, whispering to two other men who also leered with smiles close to sinister. It would appear, despite Seelios's heroics, that he still managed to have some enemies among the people of Alnerwick. Seelios considered using his ring to see if they were morally corrupt, but thought that mana would be better used at keeping the caravan alive if needed. There was always the possibility that Seelios was wrong about the stag.

The gathering at the campfire slowly shrank as people retired to their tents. Seelios couldn't help but worry that there was no real resolution to the villagers' concerns. He prayed that they could maintain their faith until they reached Paloise.

The following days were uneventful and the easiest time any of them had traveling. A flat, direct path through the forest that provided as much food as they needed was more than anyone could ask for, even though some yearned the occasional leg of lamb or turkey roast. Every once in a while they would cross paths with the Brascella River, but lose it again as it turned into the trees. It was just enough to know that the stag was still leading them to safety.

Lore told that the quickest path to a destination was as the crow flies, true and free. Most beings except birds and the Goddess of Wind, however, had to make their journey on land. Comfort was found in having a crow's sight line to the end, but to travel without clarity meant faith in success without assurance. A journey as the earthen stag walks took courage and perseverance, a test of spirit.

Some spirits were stronger than others. And when the weak broke, the whole caravan suffered.

On the fifth night of their departure from Alnerwick, the stag cleared a part of their forest for encampment, just like it had done every night before. It stood at the edge of the clearing and watched the villagers take the fruit that grew from surrounding trees and bushes. The people turned and gave their thanks, but the sincerity had grown dull.

One of the men handed Byram a handful of blackberries as he was unpacking his tent from a wagon.

"This blasted filth again?" Byram said. He glared down at the offering, then up to the man. "Enough of this. I demand real food."

Seelios walked over. "Byram, you mustn't. I know it's not—"

"Shut your mouth or I'll shut it for you. This is all your meddling fault," Byram said. He looked as if he was going to say more when his eyes drifted off Seelios's face and followed something behind him.

"Grab my hunting bow," Byram said to another villager, eyes still staring in the distance.

Seelios turned and saw a young doe sauntering along the other side of the clearing. It stopped to nibble on a cluster of red berries in the bushes. Seelios's eyes widened in horror when he saw Byram draw the string, but it was too late. Feather fletching whistled through the air as the arrow left the bow with a soft thrum. The doe's hindquarters dropped to the ground, the arrow shaft sticking from the ridge of its back. It thrashed its head about and pawed at the ground with its front legs, trying desperately to flee into the woods.

"Quick, another arrow," Byram said.

"No, stop!" Seelios said. He moved to grab the bow from the old man's hand.

"Get off me, boy, or the next arrow goes in you!"

A thunderous boom shook the ground, stilling the hearts of every person in that clearing. All heads turned to where the earthen stag once stood and saw the armored God of Earth, wielding his axe with a face of pure fury. His shining plate glittered in the light from the surrounding campfires.

"I give you shelter." Gameus stepped forward with another earth shaking stride. "I give you food." He raised his axe and the runes lit up like green flame. The surrounding trees groaned and creaked as they twisted into each other until they formed a tight wall around the perimeter of the clearing. "And I give you guidance. Yet you repay me with insolence and brutality?"

Seelios watched slender vines writhe out of the ground and wrap around the injured deer, still struggling to move on two legs. The vines squeezed and pulled the panicking animal into a hole in the ground that closed shut.

"Your contempt for the gods will not go unpunished," Gameus said. Villagers scattered away from the god as he stepped into the center of the clearing. Rending rock and crumbling earth sounded through the air as an enormous column of granite burst from the ground and lifted the God of Earth above the tree line. He looked down from his grand pedestal with disgust. "Be gone."

Seelios sprinted to his wagon, praying he would be able to stop the god before anything terrible happened. He snatched the spear and focused on the teleportation totem, disappearing in a flash of light and reappearing behind the god.

"You dare challenge me?" the god said over his shoulder.

"Gameus, spare them. They were foolish and ungrateful, but most of all they're scared," Seelios said.

Gameus narrowed his eyes. "You give me demands now? You fool. You might have some power, but you're nothing compared to me." He raised his axe again and green glowing cracks fanned out from the bottom of the column across the campground, crossing in jagged lines underneath wagons, tents, and terrified villagers. "You will watch as I send these pathetic people into the abyss of the earth."

"I won't let you." Seelios thrust his spear at the back of Gameus's green cape. The god swept his axe around and parried the spear tip with ease, turning to face Seelios. If there was any doubt before, it'd been completely erased; that axe was made out of orichalcum.

Seelios's heels were on the rock's edge and he realized there was barely enough room for the two of them on the column. The green eyes of the god were glowing with such intensity that it was hard to maintain eye contact.

"You'd sacrifice yourself for these people?" Gameus said.

"They're my responsibility. They deserve to live," Seelios said.

"You speak of such entitlement as if you were a god yourself. No one deserves to live, it is only earned. I had hopes for you, and I gave you mercy. But you bring these people through my domain and insult my hospitality. Your lack of respect is unforgivable."

Seelios's pulse was racing. Fighting a lumbering rock giant was one thing, but dueling a being who's lived for eons was entirely different.

Gameus raised his axe and the column shook. Rock crumbled beneath Seelios's feet, causing him to stumble forward to keep his balance. The god swung his axe with such speed and ferocity that Seelios hardly had time to react. He lifted his spear overhead, gripped with both hands. The blow of the axe struck with an ear piercing ring, making his arms go numb. The impact sent him flying off the column. Light enveloped Seelios in free fall and he teleported to safety before he crashed into the ground. He looked up and saw Gameus snickering down from the column.

"So you've managed to find some strength after all. I suppose those feeble limbs could use all the help they can get," the god said.

Seelios looked down at his hand. He hadn't noticed at first, but his muscles felt surged with strength. It was the only thing that kept him from crumpling under the force of Gameus's axe. He realized that he must've been using mana to increase his strength without even knowing it.

Seelios was preparing to attack Gameus again when the fissures in the ground began to split apart like ice floes in an ocean. Screams were barely audible over the rumbling of the earth as large pieces of land dropped away into a dark void below. A nearby wagon slid off the edge of a newly formed cliff and shattered into planks of timber as it tumbled and bounced. The villagers scrambled in a panicked frenzy, trying to flee through the surrounding trees which were pressed so tightly together that nothing bigger than an insect could squeeze through.

Villagers looked on in horror as black pits in the ground widened and crept ever closer. Seelios leapt over a gap and ran to a man and a woman cowering beside a wagon.

"Grab my arm," Seelios said, extending his hand. They looked confused for a moment, but didn't hesitate to comply. As soon as their hands came into contact, Seelios focused on the closest place he could think of.

When the light faded, the moonlit ruins of Alnerwick came into view. The man and the woman dropped to the ground in a tangled mess of vertigo and terror. Seelios teleported back to the campground and searched for others, grabbing anyone he could find. Some tried scrambling up trees while others hid in their wagons, hoping not to be seen. As more witnessed what Seelios was doing, they flocked to him in desperation.

Seelios tried his best to not dwell on the ones that he missed, the ones that fell into the fissures just out of reach of his finger tips. Every time he teleported back to the campground there was less earth to stand on and fewer people than he left before.

Seelios appeared in Alnerwick, easing Walter to the ground beside his fainted wife. "Please, you must find my boy!" Walter said as he collapsed to his knees. "As soon as it all started, he ran away. Gods, please let him be safe."

"I'll try," Seelios said as he disappeared in another flash.

Gameus continued to look with a wry smile from atop his column as the fissures continued to spread, causing chunks of earth to drop away into nothingness. The middle of the campground had become a hollowed abyss with a single granite spire in the middle. Seelios looked around to see if there was anyone left to save. The sea of blackness had nearly reached the trees at the edge of the clearing on all sides.

Seelios heard a young boy's cry from an abandoned wagon pushed up against the tree line. He ran over and peered inside the flaps and saw Walter's son, Elrick, huddling with the rows of immobile people inside the wagon. Panic rose inside his chest as he realized he'd forgotten about the injured. He'd forgotten about the one person who'd been protecting him up until that point; Gregory.

"Elrick, take my hand," Seelios said, reaching into the tent. The shaking ground beneath them grew more violent as the creeping abyss was nearly upon them. Gameus's booming laughter echoed off the surrounding trees.

Seelios felt the brush of a tiny hand and squeezed it in return. He dropped Elrick off in Alnerwick to the gasps of his parents and refocused back on the campground. He found his mind suddenly having trouble and realized how much he'd been using the artifact. He pulled the teleportation totem out and saw the runes had dimmed to a dull glow. There was barely any mana left within it, and he'd been draining his own life without realizing. It'd be dangerous to continue, but Gregory was still in peril.

He grasped the totem in his hand and forced his mind to focus on his destination. When he reappeared next to the wagon he landed with a thud, lungs heaving with exhaustion. He reached with a shaky hand and grasped the wooden spokes of the wheel. When he pulled himself up, he felt it sway under his weight. Gameus's abyss had nearly reached the trees and the wagon was teetering on the edge of free fall.

A hand reached out from the wagon and touched Seelios. "The totem, give it to me," Gregory said, leaning out from the back of the wagon. He looked pale skinned with dark circles under his eyes. Even after several days of rest he still looked on the brink of death.

Seelios dropped the artifact in Gregory's hand and watched as the disciple closed his eyes and scrunch his face in concentration. Beads of sweat collected on his brow, sliding down the wrinkled creases of his face and dripping off his beard. He opened his eyes and looked at Seelios with only the faintest glimmer of life left in him.

"Save . . . yourself," Gregory said. He extended a shakey hand that held the totem and another long object wrapped in cloth.

Seelios took the items and the disciple's arm swung away loosely. The teleportation totem brimmed with the tiniest amount of mana added within, just enough to make it back to Alnerwick.

The wagon groaned as the back lifted up into the air, the front teetering further over the crumbling cliff's edge. "Gregory, grab my hand!" Seelios screamed, reaching out.

Earth gave way under the weight of the wagon, and it began to tumble into free fall. Gregory reached out with a hand and smiled, mouthing goodbye, before disappearing into the empty pit.

17

G arrick spent most of his time looking at the ground as his feet walked along the forest floor. He'd grown used to seeing patches of green shrivel away from each step, as if he were a walking plague. He told himself that Seelios was right, he could go to Paloise for help. Perhaps they would execute him and release his tormented soul from this wretched life. At the very least they could imprison him and keep anyone else from harm. He would've turned around and followed the river, but he no longer had full control over his body.

"Where," Garrick whispered. "Where are we going?" He waited with a listless expression for a response, but heard nothing. Only the crunch of dead leaves and brittle twigs sounded underfoot.

The walking continued for what could've been hours or days. The concept of time was lost on him, his sanity driven away to hide from the pain. The fog of emotional void became pierced by the occasional spike of anger or sadness, neither of which he enjoyed but was better than feeling nothing at all.

"Why'd you make me do it?" Garrick said aloud. "I just . . . wanted to be with her."

"I did nothing," a voice hissed inside his head. "Your sadness and anger corrupts you. You killed her yourself."

Garrick was surprised to hear a response. The last he heard the voice was after Emeline died. He lifted his head and looked around the woods. Trees browned in decay in the wake of blight that trailed behind him.

"Show yourself," Garrick said.

"In due time," the voice said. "Once we are free."

"Then . . . how is it I can I hear—" Garrick became suddenly aware of the warmth of the crystal hanging from his neck, swinging across his chest with each step.

"Yes," the voice hissed. "You begin to understand. You carry it with you, a shard of the very prison that holds us."

"I don't want it," Garrick said. He struggled to lift his hand up to his neck. Muscles and tendons strained as his arm resisted, seeming to have a will of its own. He gave up and let his arm hang limp.

"Foolish. You and I are one, wrapped in embrace. I cannot be cast aside," the voice said.

"Leave me then, let me suffer in peace. I want nothing more of this."

The voice cackled. "Your wants matter not. A divine balance must be restored and you're going to help us."

Garrick's spine tingled with fear. He knew that something had been haunting him in his nightmares, growing more powerful with each passing day. He knew it would lead to horrible things that he could do nothing about. He knew his fate would be misery from the moment he revisited that tome in his library.

"There was a book in my possession that had seven names, telling tales of horrible deeds. Which are you?"

"Tales of horrible deeds." The voice cackled in mockery. "The books of mortals cannot begin to fathom the malevolence of our coven. I am the Bringer of Torment, the Poisoner of Minds, the Embodiment of Pestilence. Those who succumb to their hatred bend to me, just as you have and forever will. I am Abaddon, the Demon of Wrath."

THE FOREST HAD GROWN dark as the sun retreated from the sky. Garrick continued to trudge through the woods, his feet carrying him to an unknown location. The flicker of firelight shone in the distance, and Garrick thought he'd stumbled upon a camp. He prayed they would get spooked and flee before any harm came to them.

As he plodded nearer, multiple lanterns came into view, hanging from the trees. Campfires were scattered between huts built among the trunks. A village in the middle of the forest.

"Pinewood?" Garrick said.

People strolled across the rope bridges suspended between the branches. Lantern light gleamed from within abodes built high up in the canopy. As Garrick approached, a voice called out to him.

"You there, gods, you must be freezing. Where's your shirt?" a portly man said as he stepped out from a hut. He looked around curiously. "You traveling alone? Where's your horse? Mercy on your soul you must be starving, look at you. Come, have some—"

A crack echoed through the forest so loud that it seemed to frighten the whole village into silence. It was the sound of a tree breaking in half and falling to the ground, its rotten trunk no longer able to support its own weight.

"That tree stood for ages," the man said with confused look as he stared out into the woods.

Garrick continued to walk past the man and several other curious onlookers. Many villagers came out of their homes, some dressed in their bed clothes to see what the ruckus was. Many of those same people eyed Garrick with caution and concern. Mothers held their babes tight and whispered to their husbands. Garrick ignored the stares and continued onward, walking past the huts, trees, and over-hanging rope bridges.

"Whoah there, friend." A burly man with a thick beard and a large wood-axe stepped in front of Garrick.

"Get out of my way," Garrick hissed, his tone putrid and unrecognizable.

"We just want to help you, lad," the man said. "You showing up here shirtless and brooding makes these folks a bit nervous. What brings you to our parts?"

"The gods."

The burly man's eyebrows shot up at this. "Now listen here, you'll not be going nowhere near—"

Garrick reached out and grasped the man's wrist. Red swelling spread over the man's arm and down his hand, followed by a darkening of veins that created a web of black lines beneath the skin. Globules of puss burst forth and oozed out a smell of rotten meat. The burly man dropped his axe and fell to his knees, shrieking as the affliction spread up his neck and across his face. Screams rang out as people scattered into hiding.

Garrick stepped over the man thrashing about on the ground and continued walking. Bow strings twanged from overhead and arrows whistled, but he paid no attention. Something struck him in the shoulder, accompanied with a burn that felt like a wasp's sting. He looked down and saw an arrow, head buried halfway. Garrick's shoulder twitched as flesh tightened and squeezed beneath the skin until the arrow pushed out like a harmless splinter. The small wound sealed itself up in a matter of seconds. More arrows found their mark on his torso, legs, and arms. Most grazed off harmlessly while others sank in with shallow bites, only to be pushed out moments later.

"He's some kind of monster!" a voice yelled from an overhead.

"Protect the monolith," another said.

Moonlight glinted off the water's surface at the edge of the village. Men with spears and swords stood at the river's shore, blocking the head of a wide wooden dock. Towering behind them was an obelisk of stone protruding out of the water, covered in glowing blue runes.

"We must kill this abomination," one of the men said.

"Please, make this stop," Garrick whispered to himself.

"These men are between us and freedom," Abaddon's voice said. "Freedom from the gods' authoritarian rule. They must die."

"Death isn't the answer," Garrick said.

Abaddon cackled. "Death is the only answer."

Garrick felt something surge through his body, as if a ghastly hand passed through his whole being. He looked down and saw a ripple in the ground traveling away from his feet. The packed dirt cracked and broke apart. Rocks crumbled and reduced to dust and gravel. Plants and grass shrank away into nothingness. The men watched the ground with a certain panic in their eye, some backing up into the shallows of the river. When it reached their feet, their boots began to crumble away as if made of shoddy wet parchment. Their clothes tattered and fell to shreds. When their bare feet touched the tainted ground the skin blistered and cracked, oozing out blood of unnatural color. The valiant defenders collapsed into tortured screams without even raising their weapons. Some tried to jump into the river to cleanse themselves, but found no relief.

The dock groaned as Garrick walked along the wooden planks and placed his hand on the cool surface of the obelisk. Flakes of stone peeled away as the smooth gray texture turned to a spotted mold of black and white. Cracks formed and large pieces broke off and crashed into the river. The blue light of the runes faded to a dim glow, then disappeared completely. The rest of the monolith collapsed in a violent eruption of water.

"There, it is done," Garrick said.

"Not quite," Abaddon said. "We need more strength. The villagers will do nicely for a sacrifice."

18

Seelios hit the ground with harsh force, yet barely felt a thing. He rolled through thick grass before coming to rest, looking up at the starry night sky. A familiar scent of Alnerwick's farmland manure wafted into his nostrils. His body had been pushed to the limit and felt so tired that he couldn't even muster the energy to feel anything. He continued to gaze, numb to all, when a flood of tears suddenly came. His heart ached with crushing despair and he began to quietly sob. He closed his eyes to shut out the overwhelming pain, but still saw Gregory tumbling into the darkness.

Seelios jolted awake, wondering how long he'd been asleep. Galloping hooves thundered in the distance, growing louder as they drew near. Dirt and pebbles dug into his palms as he tried to push himself up, but he collapsed back onto the ground in a feeble heap. His fingers brushed something beside him. He looked down and saw the teleportation totem and the cloth wrapped object laying side by side.

The galloping drew closer as if a whole cavalry were charging his direction. Voices called to each other.

"The flash of light came from here," a man's voice said. "It must be Gregory."

Seelios lifted his head as much as his neck muscles would allow, which barely provided him a view over the stalks of grass. A small army of horsed soldiers trotted in small formation, wearing thick plates of ornate armor. The light from their torches lit up the tips of their pikes like a forest of floating knives.

"Over there, laying on the ground," a voice said from the group of soldiers.

Helmed heads turned in Seelios's direction and two men galloped over. The sudden closeness of torchlight was blinding, masking the features of the approaching men. Gasps of surprise came as the soldiers stood overhead.

"Eyes of silver. Is he a disciple?" one said.

"He's wounded," said another. "Difficult to say how bad, but conscious."

More galloping came as additional soldiers arrived. One handed his pike to the soldier next to him before he lowered himself from his horse. He knelt down beside Seelios and lifted his visor, revealing a middle-aged man with a thick, red beard.

"Can you speak? What happened here?" the bearded man said.

Seelios summoned as much energy he could and drew a breath. "The God of Earth . . . he killed so many."

The man's eyes flickered at this, a combination of confusion and fear.

The sound of another horse approaching came from behind the line of soldiers surrounding Seelios. One of the horsed soldiers turned. "M'lady, please stay with the main guard, we don't yet know if—"

"Thank you, sir, but I can handle myself," an older woman's voice said.

The horsed knight bowed his head. "Of course m'lady." He tugged his reins and trotted aside to make way.

Seelios saw a small, white-robed figure hunched over on the saddle. His eyes fell to the sun emblem on her chest, clothing identical to what Gregory wore. Seelios realized the decor of the soldiers were the same as those who helped him escape Fembleton, so valiantly giving their lives. As fate would have it, if he could not make it to Paloise, then Paloise would come to him.

The robed woman dropped down from her horse with gentle grace, her face concealed by the deep hood. She walked over to Seelios and locked eyes with him for a moment, studying him. She turned her attention to the objects on the ground. The other soldiers watched as she bent down and opened the folds of cloth. The Lumastra gleamed in her hand as she tilted it from side to side inspecting it with a careful eye.

"Where did this come from?" the woman asked as she turned back to Seelios, holding out the runic artifact. Her eyes too were a striking silver, visible even in the shadowy folds of her hood.

Seelios stared at the glass orb, a final reminder of the friend that he'd lost.

"The man who had this, where is he now?" she asked.

Seelios closed his eyes and fought back more tears. "Gone," he whispered. "Gameus killed him and many others."

"Then it's true," the woman said to herself. She turned to

the main group of soldiers. "Raphael, come. This boy needs healing."

Seelios lifted his head to see another horse trot over, carrying two people. The one in front was a pike-wielding knight while the second was another hooded white-robed disciple. The horse stopped beside the woman and the robed man slowly lowered himself off the saddle, struggling half-way down.

"Confound it, soldier. Help me down," Raphael said, struggling to stretch his leg to the ground.

"Y—yes, m'lord," the knight said. He turned in the saddle and held the robed man as he made his slow descent, wincing a bit as his left leg came to rest on the dirt.

The sun emblem became visible when he straightened out his robes. He thrust out an open palm toward the knight. "Well? You don't expect me to hobble around without support, do you?"

The knight paused, then moved in small, flustered motions as if he were thinking of what he was supposed to do. Finally, he offered his pike to the disciple.

"I supposed that'll do," Raphael said as he grabbed the pike and used it brace himself as he walked. He hobbled across the grass and stood over Seelios, looking down at him. It was a haunting sight to see two sets of silvery eyes staring through shadowy hoods.

The hunched woman turned to the surrounding soldiers. "Leave us."

"Wait. There are others in the town with nowhere to go. Please, help them," Seelios said.

One of the knights nodded and, without a word, they galloped away. Silence passed between Seelios and the two disciples as they waited for the hoof beats to go silent, falling back into formation with the rest of the escort.

Seelios tried to sit up, but the muscles in his abdomen gave out before he'd even reached halfway. He slumped back down on the grass in helpless resignation.

"Calm yourself, boy," Raphael said as he slowly crouched down, like an old man with aching joints. "Injure yourself more and you make it harder for the both of us."

The disciple extended a palm from his robes and pressed it on Seelios's chest. The warmth from his touch spread, sinking down into aching muscle. Seelios had experienced the healing sensation of a rejuvenation stone, but it was nothing compared to Raphael's power. There was no pain from wounds stitching back together or bones rejoining. The feeling was soothing and gentle, like dipping into a warm bath on a cold day.

"Such fragility. Curious though, you've taken much damage yet your wounds are superficial," Raphael said. He reached into his robes and pulled out a leather bound book and quill. The feather wiggled in the air as the disciple scratched a few short notes then snapped it closed.

"That should do," Raphael said as he stood with the assistance of the pike.

The whole process had taken mere seconds, an instant compared to Seelios using the rejuvenation stone. With nothing more than a small touch from the disciple, Seelios felt like his injuries were completely gone. He blinked for a moment and sat up with ease. He flexed his hands and looked down at his arms. Dry blood still glistened in the moonlight, but the scratches had disappeared. He was far from being in top shape, but was no longer close to death.

Seelios looked at Raphael, peering at the eyes in the hood.

"You have a rejuvenation stone? Gregory didn't mention there were others," Seelios said.

A soldier came galloping up to them.

"M'lady, m'lord, please pardon the interruption," the armored knight said. "There are a handful of survivors in the town as the boy said. They claim the boy saved them from the God of Earth."

The two disciples turned to each other for a moment and gave small nods. Raphael reached up and drew his hood back. Surprisingly, he wasn't the old man Seelios had imagined. He was middle-aged with short brown hair, a long nose, and clean-shaven. Oddly enough, the man looked somewhat familiar. Seelios drew in a sharp breath of sudden realization when it dawned on him.

"That frightening, am I?" Raphael said.

"Sorry, no. It's just, I've seen you before," Seelios said.

Raphael frowned at this. "I think I might recall a scrawny thing like you walking around Paloise."

Seelios shook his head. "No, here in Alnerwick. At least, it wasn't you, but rather someone that looked like you. The God of Earth commands men of clay and gives them faces. A few days ago many were in the village and . . . yours was one of them."

Raphael brought a hand up to his chin in curious thought. "Very strange indeed. I can't say I've ever met the Lord of the Earth before." He pulled out his book and scribbled more notes.

"Tell me of Gregory. What did he say to you?" the woman said.

Seelios nodded. "He came to Fembleton to give news about a gate to my father."

"Gregory would not share that lightly. He must've had great trust in you," she said.

Raphael turned to her. "The boy's eyes . . . Mirabelle, this must be who we felt."

She drew her hood back, revealing the old wrinkled face of an elderly woman. Her silver eyes had laugh lines around them, giving her a friendly appearance despite her serious expression. Her white hair was pulled back and hung down in a thick braid.

"We must be sure." Mirabelle turned to Seelios. "What is your name?"

"I'm Seelios."

The disciples stared at him. Raphael raised an eyebrow in expectation and leaned his head forward, beckoning for more.

"I meant, Seelios Strongheart of Fembleton, son of Ricker Strongheart."

Mirabelle considered the words for a moment, nodding. "You're very lucky we found you," she said. "Besides the few survivors in the town, are there any others?"

"There were," Seelios said as he looked down. "But they didn't make it."

"Where?" Raphael asked as he twisted his head, looking about. "I see no bodies."

Seelios raised a finger and pointed to the forest. Raphael turned to Mirabelle with an expectant look, one single eyebrow raised.

Mirabelle raised her open palms upward, cupped next to each other, and a soft glow began to emanate from them. A gentle wisp of light gathered into a ball that floated above her hands, no brighter than a coal ember. The wisp hovered over their heads for a moment, then drifted off, illuminating the trunks and leaves of the forest as it swept across the tree line. The light vanished when it disappeared into the caravan tunnel created by the earthen stag.

Seelios watched Mirabelle, who closed her eyes and looked as if she was in deep focus. Several moments passed, then her face grimaced with pain and sorrow. "Such unwonted destruction. There is a pit that sinks a great distance. What Seelios says is true. Many people died here, including Gregory."

She opened her eyes and took several deep breaths, as if regaining her composure.

"The God of Earth has turned, then?" Raphael asked.

Mirabelle shook her head. "It's unclear. We need to return to Paloise right away."

Raphael turned to the soldiers and raised his pike, waggling it in the air. Three knights rode over, trailing an unmanned horse with them.

"Can you ride?" Raphael asked Seelios.

Seelios nodded. "In my childhood I often rode a donkey and—"

Raphael scoffed at him with disbelief and disgust. "Donkey?" He looked to the horse, then to Seelios. "Does that look like a donkey to you?"

"No, I was just saying—"

Raphael waved a dismissive hand and turned to Mirabelle. "Are we really bothering with him? His intelligence is questionable."

Mirabelle frowned at Raphael. "Don't be harsh." She turned to Seelios. "It's fine if you aren't familiar with horses, it'll be a short trip."

Seelios decided not to push the issue further and went to the empty horse, hooked his leg in the stirrups, and swung onto the saddle. He knew the distance from Alnerwick to Paloise was several days of riding. Maybe the concept of a short trip was different to a Disciple of Light.

Two soldiers helped Raphael into his saddle. The look on his face seemed as if he didn't enjoy the prospect of hugging another man to stay secure. In fairness, being a powerful disciple seemed to command a certain level of stature that didn't quite match the visual of his feebleness.

Mirabelle motioned for Seelios to come beside her. They started riding together toward the main guard and the others fell behind them. The larger group of knights split and let Seelios and the disciples through. They rolled around and fell in line behind.

Seelios leaned back in his saddle as his horse charged down the slope of a hill. At the bottom, he saw a sea of torchlights so vast it could've been a projection of the night sky. Another army lay waiting, much larger than the cohort that found Seelios.

"I didn't know Paloise had so many soldiers," Seelios said to Mirabelle.

"There had been word of the destruction of Fembleton and Alnerwick," she said with a hint of sadness in her voice. "We came as soon as we could, but the message took several days to reach us."

"We're close, then?" Seelios asked, surprised.

"No, but we have the means to travel great distances if need be, as you are aware."

The army of knights at the bottom of the hill also bore pikes and other weapons such as crossbows, battle-axes, and war hammers. Scattered throughout their massive formation were several large supply wagons.

Mirabelle took the lead in front of Seelios and the knights parted for them as they galloped toward a large carriage covered in thick metal armor. The thing must have weighed a ton, which explained the four enormous horses that were hitched to its front.

Mirabelle stopped her horse and climbed down. Seelios did the same and the two of them waited for Raphael as knights ran to help him down from his horse. He waved them away and grabbed the knight's pike again, hobbling over to where Mirabelle and Seelios stood. The three of them walked around to the back of the armored carriage where a guard stood watch. He straightened when Mirabelle came into his view and opened a heavy door that squealed on iron hinges. Mirabelle lifted herself up into the carriage. Raphael followed with the help of the guard.

Seelios stood outside, looking at the lantern glow that came through the door. He turned and found a row of soldiers surrounding him. The door guard made a terse gesture for Seelios to go inside. It was beginning to feel like he was no longer being rescued, but being captured.

Seelios pursed his lips and forced a smile, then lifted himself into the carriage doorway. The inside walls were lined with plush velvet cushioning adorned with gold fastenings. The ceiling had small, dangling lanterns that were chained together with strands of crystals.

Raphael settled onto a thick cushion, wincing in pain as he bent his legs into a cross-legged position. Mirabelle was seated in similar fashion, leaning down toward another man who was lying on a bed, draped in a thick quilt decorated with an intricate patterned weave of gold and silver.

"Seelios, come here," Mirabelle said as she patted a cushion next to her.

Seelios stepped into the carriage and the door slammed shut behind him with a metallic clang, followed by the click of a bolt locking into place. Grasping his hands over his pockets, he felt for the teleportation totem, then realized Mirabelle had it.

"We know what this might seem like. There must be certain precautions," Mirabelle said. "Now, please, sit with us."

Seelios looked from Mirabelle to Raphael, who looked

as if he were growing more impatient by the moment. The man lying in the bed watched Seelios intently. He was a man who looked to be in his thirties with darker skin, short black hair, and a small goatee. His silver eyes blazed at Seelios from across the carriage.

At least three disciples had ridden from Paloise to investigate something with a whole army at their back. Perhaps a war truly was coming.

Seelios strode across the wood planks of the carriage floor to the cushion beside Mirabelle. He settled down cross-legged like the others.

"Come now, let's get on with it," Raphael said, his impatience seeming to spill over to anger.

Mirabelle gave a gentle smile. "For a Disciple of Light you lack a surprising amount of tolerance."

Raphael narrowed his eyes. "There is much work to do at the temple." He turned to the disciple lying in the bed. "On with it, Michael."

The dark skinned man sat up from his pillow and looked into Seelios's eyes. "So this is the boy," he said, looking him up and down with a furrowed brow. "Such fragility."

Seelios looked down and noticed that Michael was missing his left hand, a smooth stump of skin in its place. If the disciples had the power to heal it was a wonder why they didn't use it on themselves. Seelios felt shame at the insensitivity of the thought and looked up from Michael's arm.

"Will we be riding the rest of the way to Paloise in this?" Seelios asked.

None of them answered. They looked at him with calculating glances.

Mirabelle turned to Michael. "Can you do it with all four

of us? Even after the whole army?"

Michael scrunched his face slightly, deep in concentration. "Yes," he said after a moment.

Mirabelle reached out and grabbed Seelios's reluctant hand. "Worry not, we mean you no harm," she said. She pulled his hand over and joined with Michael's. Raphael leaned over from his cushion and placed a hand on Michael's shoulder.

A familiar etching of runes began to glow from the inside Michael's robes, so bright that they shone through like it was made of a sheer material. He looked up at Seelios with a smile. "You are familiar with teleportation totems?"

Seelios nodded.

"Then let us go."

Everything disappeared in a flood of light, and Seelios felt the floor beneath him disappear.

SEELIOS HAD USED his own teleportation totem several times, some instances to travel long distances and some to travel short. Just when he thought he was getting used to the sensation, he'd been caught by overwhelming vertigo as he tumbled through space in a vacuum of light. The feeling of being a passenger in teleportation was entirely different. The closest sensation he could relate it to was free-falling through the air with no indication when the landing would come. It was no wonder all of the villagers were so disoriented when he took them back to Alnerwick.

A smooth, white stone floor faded into view. There was no fall, no harsh landing, just the gentle appearance of ground beneath him. Seelios found himself resting on his hands and knees, trying to still the spinning of his head. He slowly lifted his eyes to take in his surroundings. The room was a small, yet cozy bedroom fit for someone of noble birth. A large canopied bed lay in the center with swirling vines and flowers carved into the wood. Fine mahogany furniture lined the stone wall, including an open wardrobe containing a suite of fine robes, shirts, pants, and other articles of clothing. Iron sconces held lit torches that cast a warm light about the room.

Seelios continued to admire the decor when his drifting gaze found the disciples watching him with calculating stares. Mirabelle and Raphael stood behind Michael, who was seated in a chair that sat atop a platform of wheels.

"Where am I?" Seelios asked.

Mirabelle gestured to a tall, open window. "Why don't you see for yourself?"

Seelios got to his feet and walked to the wall. The vast moon hung just above the horizon, the largest he'd ever seen. It radiated with a crisp blue aura so beautiful that it pulled at Seelios's heart, shining over a layer of wispy white clouds. He leaned out the window and the chilly night air whipped over his golden hair. The stone wall stretched out below him until it disappeared into a distant fog. A small gap in the drifting clouds revealed a silver line of water snaking through hills and forest. The Brascella River, one of the great life lines of Inf, reduced to a mere stitching in the cloth of the earth.

He felt his vertigo coming back and stepped away from the window. He looked at the disciples. "This is Paloise?"

"Yes," Mirabelle said. "We are in a room nearly at the top of Ophanim's Grand Temple, built in honor of the God of Light and home to the disciples."

Seelios whispered to himself, "I'm finally here." He turned to Mirabelle. "I thought I'd imagined this tower. I saw it, glowing in the distance."

Raphael chuckled. "Impossible. No one can see this tower."

"No one except us," Mirabelle said with a smile, wagging a finger at Raphael.

Raphael snorted and looked away, annoyed.

"Get some rest. Tomorrow will be a long day," Michael said. "I'm sorry to say, but we will be needing your remaining artifacts." He held out an open palm.

Seelios was expecting this at some point, surprised they didn't ask before. Some part of him still hoped that they'd forget, he already felt naked without the teleportation totem. He pulled the inert rejuvenation stone from his pocket and dropped it into Michael's hand.

Michael cleared his throat. "I believe you're forgetting one."

Seelios frowned in concentration as he thought. "No, I gave you all—" He looked down at the ring on his hand, then back up to Michael with eyes wide. "You can't mean this. It was a gift from my father. Please, be reasonable."

Michael gave an impatient look and beckoned with the fingers of his still outstretched palm.

Seelios slid off the ring and gave it a longing look as he gave it to Michael. The disciple retracted his hand and gave a solemn nod to the other disciples by his side. Mirabelle shuffled behind his chair and pushed it to the door. Raphael followed, clicking a gnarled wooden cane as he hobbled.

"What is tomorrow?" Seelios asked.

"The beginning of your deliberations," Michael said over his shoulder, just before the door pulled shut.

Seelios looked around the room. It might have all the comforts that Paloise had to offer, but it was clear that he was in nothing more than a beautiful prison.

19

Despite being imprisoned in a fortified tower, Seelios experienced luxuries he'd never dreamed of. The canopied bed was the more comfortable than anything Fembleton had to offer. A young hand maiden visited his room in the morning, leading him to a room down the hall that had a large tub filled with steaming bath water. Soaking in clean water scented with hints of lilac, he could've spent the entire day lounging in that tub. The meals had sweet fruits, savory meats, and the most delectable bread that he'd ever tasted.

Even with the distraction of such extravagance, thoughts of suffering intruded his mind. The townsfolk of Alnerwick, Garrick, Emeline, Gregory; they were all brought into harm's way because of Seelios. For the past several days Seelios thought the only thing that mattered was to safely get to Paloise. Now that he was there, he realized there was no satisfaction to be had. There was no sense that he'd done the right thing, only destruction and death seemed to travel in his wake.

A whole day passed of him sitting in his room, alone except for the occasional visit of the hand maiden. She was no help when he asked questions about why he was being kept or when the disciples would come back. The next morning Seelios watched the sunrise come up over tiny forested hills and a layer of clouds that stretched into the horizon. Unable to sleep the entire night, he had spent countless hours perched at that window, gazing across the stratosphere.

A jingling noise came from the other side of the wall as someone fumbled for a key before jamming it into the door. A heavy bolt slid to the side and the door creaked open. A large woman wearing the disciple's white robes filled the entire frame. Her wide face held an intimidating gaze, framed with short brown hair. Her stout figure made her look like she could wrestle a bull. She walked in, followed by two more white robed figures. Seelios immediately recognized the hunched stature and smiling facade of Mirabelle. The other was a man who looked to be no older than his late twenties. He had long black hair that concealed part of a pale face and was younger than any other disciple Seelios had seen. He wondered how many disciples there actually were.

"I hope you've found your quarters comfortable," Mirabelle said with a wrinkled smile. "This is Anysia." She gestured to the large woman standing beside her. "And this is Adriel." Mirabelle pointed to the skinny black haired man, who seemed to be shifting his gaze to look anywhere except Seelios's eyes.

"This," Anysia looked Seelios up and down, "is the boy you spoke of?" She turned to Mirabelle as she inflected the end of her question.

Mirabelle nodded, continuing to look at Seelios. "It is.

He has already proven to have some knowledge of mana and runic artifacts. He also claims to have pierced the illusion."

Anysia raised her eyebrow, then looked at Adriel. "In the centuries I've been a disciple, never has this tower been revealed. Is this your responsibility or Alodia's?"

Adriel gave a deep sigh and whipped his black hair out of his face. "The illusion has remained."

"Seelios didn't see it by chance," Mirabelle said. "I believe he's achieved a mastery over his truth ring."

Anysia snorted a breath and shook her head. "Such a thing isn't possible." She curled her lip. "Taught to him by someone who didn't even have that kind of mastery himself. Gregory wouldn't be able to show the boy this." She turned to Seelios. "And you say you witnessed his death?"

Seelios lowered his head. "Yes."

"How did he die?"

Seelios shifted his feet and looked back up at the disciples. "The God of Earth attacked us. Gregory died saving me."

Adriel's head snapped in Seelios's direction, black hair swirling through the air. Intensity blazed in his silver eyes. "A god would never do such a thing."

"I . . . I thought so too, but that wasn't the first time he attacked. The first was Fembleton, my hometown, then Alnerwick," Seelios said.

Anysia narrowed her eyes. "The more you talk, the less makes sense. The God of Earth would never stray so far from his own realm. Your lies are obvious."

Seelios felt a pang of annoyance. "I'm telling the truth. Why would I lie about that?"

Anysia brought her hand up, revealing a silver ring

encrusted with gems. Runes lit up across its surface and shone with yellow light.

"His aura isn't pure," Anysia said, staring at Seelios with glowing eyes.

"He can learn. He's endured much hardship. His heart needs time to heal," Mirabelle said.

"Don't be so quick to trust him," Anysia said, lowering her hand. Light faded from her eyes and her cold silver eyes remained on Seelios. "How is it you survived two attacks from the God of Earth?"

"Three, actually. Gregory protected me. We fled, but he discovered us in Alnerwick," Seelios said. "We were trying to come to Paloise. Gregory said it was important that I made it, so I could meet all of you."

"The god then found you and your caravan in the forest in the middle of the night?" Anysia asked.

"Not exactly. The god was actually leading us here." Seelios drifted off to a whisper with his last word, knowing how the story must've sounded.

Anysia's eyebrows shot up in surprise. "Did I hear you correctly?"

"W—wait, allow me to explain. Gameus, he said I'm important for something. That there's a war coming and I—"

Anysia held up a hand, her face contorted into fury. "Cease your yammering. It has become clear that you spin lies at your convenience." She turned, shaking her head with a look of disgust, and walked out of the room. Mirabelle looked at Seelios for a moment, studying him with a calculating expression, before following Anysia.

"Please, it's not how it sounds. I know it doesn't make sense, but you must listen," Seelios said.

Adriel stepped after them but stopped just before the

door. He turned to Seelios. "You're familiar with using runic artifacts I've heard. How well do you wield an illusion amulet?"

"I . . . don't know what that is," Seelios said.

Adriel reached his hand into the neckline of his robe and pulled up a necklace with a circular orichalcum pendant carved like a sun. As it dangled from his hand, parts of the charm faded in and out, like an oasis on the horizon of a hot desert. Adriel pursed his lips and held an impatient look on his face, waiting for an answer. Seelios studied it for a moment, then frowned. The black haired disciple gave a disappointed grunt and walked out the door, slamming it closed behind him.

Seelios was stunned. It might have been stress or the lack of sleep, but it seemed like everything he said somehow came out wrong.

A FEW HOURS had passed since Mirabelle and the others visited Seelios's room. He spent his time waiting, wandering about, trying to distract his mind as best as he could. He tried anything to keep from the mounting anxiety, even taking some time to browse through the wardrobe. As expected, many of the pants, tunics, shirts, and jackets were too large for him.

He'd just donned a green tunic when a flash of light filled the room, followed by a scorching heat wave. The skin of Seelios's neck and arms felt like they were on fire, and he dove behind the bed to get out of the painful light. The entire room was bright, but the source of the light seemed to be coming the center of the floor.

When the radiance faded Seelios wondered if he'd escaped a harsh judgment at the hands of Anysia, attempting to disintegrate him with the power of light. Still, he thought the power of the Lumastra was stronger. Surely half of the room would've been missing.

Seelios heard the sound of shuffling feet over stone and knew that someone was in his room. The burning scent of smoke permeated the air.

"A fine job you did nearly setting the whole room ablaze," a man's voice said.

"I— I'm sorry, I don't know what happened. I'm better than that," a younger man's voice said. It could've belonged to a teenager.

"I'll tell you what happened. You lost your focus and couldn't control the artifact. Look at this place," the older voice said. "Young man, are you in here? Gods, if you destroyed our only— look there, put that out."

Seelios slowly peeked his head up over the bed and saw a young disciple with long brown hair rushing over to a pile of leaflets that had caught aflame on the desk.

"Not just that. Look here," Michael said. He was sitting in his wheeled chair in the middle of the room, pointing at the glowing red edges of decorative lace that was shrinking away like a lit fuse. The younger disciple ran over and began batting it with a cloth. His eyes went wide when he spotted Seelios standing up on the other side of the bed and began to back away. He regained his composure and stood by Michael, straightening himself upright.

"Ah, Seelios. We do apologize for the extremely intrusive," Michael gave the young disciple a small glare, "entrance. It would appear our young adept here is even more novice in teleportation than I'd realized."

The younger disciple's face reddened to near crimson.

"Please," Seelios said as he circled around the bed,

"before you ask me questions like the others, can you tell me why I'm here?"

Michael stroked his chin as he pondered for a moment. "I suppose the customs of the Disciples of Light are lost on those who live in the country lands. Much knowledge has been shared with you. Too much, in fact, without the full approval of the rest of the disciples."

"But, Gregory taught me. If he trusted me enough, doesn't that mean anything?" Seelios said.

"And is he here to verify his approval of your training?" Michael said.

Seelios went quiet. There was nothing he could say to that.

"Come," Michael said as he beckoned Seelios over.

The stone floor was still warm as Seelios crossed the room to where the disciples were.

Michael extended an open palm facing up at the young disciple, who returned with a look of surprise through his long strands of brown hair.

"Master, I can do it," the boy said.

Michael shot a look that would've melted Seelios into the wall. "Now, Gabriel."

A look of shame crossed over the young teenager's face as he reached into the sleeve of his robe and pulled out a small statue of carved marble, shaped somewhat like an hour glass. He placed it in Michael's palm and the artifact brightened into radiance at his touch, runes springing to life like they had been freshly branded.

"Come, just like in the carriage," Michael said.

Seelios stepped closer and put a hand on Michael's shoulder. Gabriel did the same on Michael's other shoulder. A soft glow enveloped them and Seelios felt his feet leave the ground.

When the light faded and his feet felt a solid touch, he found himself staring out into an endless blue sky dotted with puffy white clouds. Bright sunlight shone directly onto him from overhead and a gentle breeze wrapped around Seelios like a warm hug. He looked down saw that his feet were mere inches away from the edge of the floor, which dropped off into nothing but an ocean of sky. He was standing on large stone platform with no walls or ceiling.

"Quite spectacular, isn't it?" Michael said.

Seelios turned and saw Michael and Gabriel in the middle of the platform. Beneath them was a large mosaic sun crafted into the stone. Its complex pattern of alternating whites, oranges, reds, and blues created a breath taking work of art.

"It's beautiful," Seelios said as he looked out to the sky. Nothing but clouds and infinite blue could be seen, even in the perfect clarity of the day. It made Seelios's palms sweaty to think about how high up they were. A brisk wind could blow him clean off and leave him tumbling through the air for hours.

"It is a place where only the Disciples of Light can come. As you can see, there are no stairs or any other means to get up here," Michael said. "This is where you'll be receiving your judgment."

Seelios stiffened. He wasn't sure what that meant and waited for the disciple to continue.

"Do you think you are strong enough?" Gabriel asked. He snickered a bit as he made the comment, flipping his hair out of his face as the breeze flailed it about.

"Yes," Seelios said in as defiant a voice as he could muster.

Michael narrowed his eyes. "You do not look strong. And

from what Anysia has told me, your resolve can be quite weak."

Seelios took a step toward Michael. "I stood up to the God of Earth to save—"

"And you failed," Michael said.

Anger was beginning to build in Seelios's chest, but he stayed his tongue.

Glowing light filled Michael's eyes as he stared deep into Seelios's soul. He held his gaze for a few moments as Seelios stared back, determined to maintain eye contact.

The light faded from Michael's eyes and he gave Seelios a thoughtful look.

"Come, it is time to take you back," Michael said.

SEELIOS SAT at the desk in his room in Ophanim's tower, scratching away with a quill at the leaflets that hadn't been burned up by Gabriel's chaotic teleportation. The flickering sconces and moonlight had become old friends, keeping him company on his sleepless nights while he waited for the next visit.

Two days had passed since any disciple set foot in the room and the only interaction since was with the shy handmaiden. She still never said a word to Seelios, despite his insisting questions about what was happening and when he would see the next disciple.

When a knock came at the door, Seelios assumed it was his lunch being delivered.

"Just leave it inside the door," Seelios called out. He'd grown irritable and tired, knowing that if he saw the girl again that he would just end up screaming his questions in frustration. Seelios had never been one to surround himself with a large score of people, but he'd come to find that confinement and solitude did not suit him.

The door creaked open. "I am not your handmaiden," a deep, gruff voice said.

Seelios spun in his chair and saw one of the biggest men he'd ever laid eyes on, standing at the arch of the door frame. With curly blond hair, a short light brown beard, and huge rippling muscles visible even under the folds of the disciple's robe, he reminded Seelios of Garrick, except much larger. He stooped down and turned his shoulders to enter.

As the large disciple stood up again, Seelios noticed that he held the Lumastra in his massive hand. His heart began to race at the thought of that weapon being used on him. Perhaps that was what was meant by receiving his judgment.

Seelios was in the middle of imagining the sensation of getting blasted with a lethal beam of light when he saw a young woman stride into the room. Her long black hair flowed with each step, framing a face of perfect features. Her eyes sparkled with the same silver light of all the other disciples, yet captivated Seelios with a lively fire that burned within them. She was hauntingly beautiful, and had Seelios mesmerized to the point of completely forgetting about his imagined demise.

The large disciple cleared his throat, snapping Seelios back to his senses.

"I'm Harut," the large man said. "This is Alodia."

The girl with the long black hair smiled at Seelios, mostly with her eyes, making her beauty all the more enchanting.

"It's nice to meet you. I'm glad you didn't storm in like the last two," Seelios said as he stood up from his chair.

"Pardon?" Harut asked.

Seelios waved his hand, embarrassed. "Never mind."

Harut frowned at the gesture, and Seelios realized that he was being too casual. Nerves raised, Seelios gestured to a set of chairs at a table. "Would you like to sit?"

Harut looked at the chairs. "Afraid not."

Seelios looked at the wooden chairs, lined with plush cushions. Of course they were too small, they would've barely been big enough to seat an average adult. He felt a panic begin to rise in his chest, knowing that he was only offending the disciple more with each passing moment.

A shiver of movement came from Alodia and Seelios noticed that she held the back of her hand up to her mouth, stifling a laugh. She brought it down and had a smile spread across her face. Seelios returned the smile for a brief moment.

Harut raised an eyebrow and looked at Alodia, then back to Seelios. He shrugged and held up the Lumastra for Seelios. "You recognize this artifact?"

Seelios nodded.

"Have you used it?" Harut asked.

"No, Gregory forbade it. He said I would need proper training."

Harut frowned and studied Seelios for a moment. "Wise. Could kill yourself if you're not ready." He looked down the Lumastra, then to Seelios. "Would you like to try?"

Seelios felt taken aback, opening his mouth to say something in polite rejection, but realized he always did want to try it. He stood motionless, not sure what to say.

Harut smiled and extended out the handle of the artifact. Seelios slowly took it in his hand and hefted it. The orb gleamed at the top and the orichalcum strips warmed to the touch. The faintest etching of runes grew alight.

Seelios looked up and saw the two disciples watching

him with heavy anticipation. They barely knew him, yet they handed him a powerful god-forged weapon and expected him to figure out how to use it. He wondered if that's what it was like being a Disciple of Light, expected to do miraculous things with little guidance.

Harut motioned to the sun-filled window. "Please, if you feel you are ready."

The sky looked bright and sunny, but as Seelios stepped up to the window's edge he noticed the dark gray cloud that carpeted below. If he'd been on the surface it would've been a dreadful, rainy day.

"Aim above the horizon, if you will," Harut said.

Alodia turned to Harut. "Are you sure? If he manages to drop his aim a little bit below—"

"Have faith in the boy, won't you? Let us give the citizens of Paloise a light show."

Seelios turned back to the window. He held out the Lumastra at arms length, pointing it up at an angle. He closed his eyes and let his mind search out the runic artifact. The familiarity of its energy met him like a long lost friend, distant but not forgotten. There were many strange complexities about the artifact, but Seelios was beginning to feel confident he could use it. He opened his eyes and saw that the runes were blazing with bright intensity. The mana surged along the orichalcum bands, free and ready to be disposed as its wielder wished. He wrapped his mind over the stored mana and pushed it to the orb where it began to glimmer like a star.

A sharp gasp came from Alodia and Seelios felt a jolt of pride and excitement. Brimming with confidence, he pushed the rest of the mana into the orb and it flashed with an erratic burst. Light cascaded out its sides, shooting out in a spread rather than a focused beam. Light ripped through the bottom of the arch of the window, blasting away blocks of stone like pebbles in a hurricane.

Seelios backed away and dropped the Lumastra to the ground with a ring.

Harut cursed loudly and picked up the artifact. "Go to Raphael and Michael. There will be healing needed."

Alodia rushed out in a flash of black hair, disappearing out the door and up the stairs. Seelios turned back to the window, which looked like something had exploded on the sill. Large chunks of rock were missing, leaving jagged edges that went nearly to the floor.

Harut stomped out of the room and slammed the door closed behind him.

SEELIOS LAY on his bed for hours, sick to his stomach at the thought of hurting anyone else. He prayed that the disciples were able to save those that needed it.

The door burst open and a cacophony of bickering flooded the room. Raphael hobbled in with his cane, rambling with another disciple with darker skin and short black hair. They moved to the table, shouting at each other in what appeared to be an argument. They took their seats and spread out a shuffle of parchments in front of them.

Raphael's face scrunched up with irritation. "You confounded idiot, it would never work that way. You'd have to—"

"The orichalcum is the key, Raphael. Don't you see? It needs to reflect the light more. The metallurgy needs to be worked," the other disciple said in a calmer, but still raised, voice.

Raphael began shaking his head. "No. The light must be absorbed, then transferred."

The other disciple considered for a moment, then brightened. "Perhaps we could have two devices, one to gather and one to discharge. Write that down." He waggled a finger at the table.

Raphael's lip turned up. "One of the most brilliant minds in the temple and you can't even remember to bring a parchment and quill with you? Gods forbid you come up with an idea when you're by yourself." He mumbled to himself as a scribbled on one of the parchments, tore off a portion, and tossed it across the table.

"What was it we came for?" Raphael said as he looked around the room. His eyes fell on Seelios, who'd been watching on with curiosity.

"Right, of course," Raphael said with a groan. "You're fortunate your little accident happened while it was raining. All the fires were extinguished by the time we'd arrived."

"Was anyone hurt?" Seelios asked.

"Besides a couple having the daylights scared out of them when a piece of our temple smashed through their ceiling, no."

Seelios breathed a heavy sigh of relief. Having the Disciples of Light think him to be even more incompetent was something he could live with, but more people getting hurt was more than he could bear.

Raphael stood from his chair, bracing himself with his cane. He motioned for the other disciple to speak. "Well, go on."

The darker skinned disciple stood up, gathering the parchments off the table. He held them up, looking from one to the other as if he were searching for something. His eyes lit up and he dropped all of the parchments back on the table except for one.

Seelios watched the disciple walk the scroll over to the

bed and hold it out. It had a sketch of what looked like a fanciful centerpiece for a grand dining table. It most resembled a flower with metallic petals curling upward, cradling a large faceted gem in its center. Sketched lines with different scribbles of measurements criss-crossed over the design. Notes were scattered all over the document, crossed out, erased, and reworded to the point of illegibility.

The disciple tapped the parchment with a finger. "Tell me what you think."

Seelios blinked at the design, overwhelmed. "It's impressive."

The disciple turned his head to Raphael and smiled, jerking a thumb at Seelios. "You see?"

Raphael rolled his eyes. "Maalik, the boy doesn't know a horse from a donkey."

Maalik turned back to Seelios. "You know what this is, don't you?"

"A runic artifact?"

A smile grew across Maalik's face. "Yes. Yes it is." A silence filled the air as Maalik looked at Seelios with anticipation, his smile growing wider.

Seelios looked down at the parchment, then up to Maalik's broad grin. "Was there . . . something else?"

"Don't you see it?" Maalik said.

"I'm not sure what you mean."

Maalik's smiled began to fade and he pointed at the design. "The calculations. They're all wrong. You know what they should be, correct?"

Seelios gave a nervous glance over to Raphael, who was looking on with smug boredom.

"I'm sorry," Seelios said as he looked back to Maalik. "I'm afraid I don't."

Maalik looked at Seelios with disbelief.

"You see, Maalik? Wouldn't believe me, would you?" Raphael said.

"But, your mind. It's supposed to be—"

Raphael shushed him. "Don't be foolish, we can't entrust him with any more secrets. He's too dangerous."

Disbelief and confusion still on his face, Maalik walked over to the table and gathered up all the remaining parchment in his arms. He mumbled to himself inaudibly as he walked out the door. Raphael followed him, clicking his cane with every other step.

A FULL DAY had passed since the strange encounter with Maalik and Raphael, interrupted only by the delivery of his meals. He could tell the food was incredibly delicious, but his emotions kept him so distant that he wasn't able to enjoy the taste. The only thing he could think of was the disciples deliberating his terrible fate in a far off chamber.

That night was the first in many that he'd actually drifted off to sleep. Despite his exhaustion, what haunted him in his dreams made him wish he were still awake. His nightmares were plagued with visions of terrified villagers, chased and killed by Gameus's minions.

Gregory, laying on the wagon just after he'd given Seelios the Lumastra, was the last image he saw before he woke. Seelios opened his eyes and the bed's dark canopy hung above, dimly lit only by the moonlight. A breeze rolled in through the open window, chilling him to the bone. His shirt was matted to his chest and he realized he was drenched in sweat.

Seelios had just finished changing into another set of clothes when a soft knock came at the door. He thought he imagined it, a lingering part of his dreams. He thought it odd that anyone would come to meet him in the middle of the night.

Another knock came, louder than before.

Adrenaline shook Seelios from his drowsiness and he walked over to the door. When he opened it, there was another disciple holding a lit candle, filling the doorway with dim, orange light.

"Eyes of silver, so it is true. I had to see it for myself," the disciple said, staring intently at Seelios. "May I come in?" He was an older man of average size with brown hair and a short beard speckled with white. He had a solemn air about him as the light flickered over his face. There was a familiar look to him, but Seelios couldn't pinpoint it.

Seelios stepped aside and held the door open. "Of course. I was already awake,"

The disciple walked in and began to light the sconces around the wall. "At this hour?"

"I haven't been sleeping too well. Nightmares come to me," Seelios said as he closed the door.

"What about?" The disciple lit the last sconce, walked to the table, and seated himself in one of the chairs.

Seelios walked over and sat across from him. "Death and suffering of people that I could've saved."

A glow came from the disciples hand, and Seelios saw the runes of a truth ring illuminate.

"You carry sorrow with you," the disciple said from behind glowing eyes. The light quickly faded and he slipped off the ring, placing it in the middle of the table. He gestured toward it. "Go on. This one is yours after all."

Seelios looked down at the table and recognized the stone band. He regarded the disciple for a moment, wondering why they'd give him the artifact back all of a sudden. He slowly reached out with his hand and picked up the ring.

"On one condition," the disciple said.

Seelios froze his hand mid-air.

"You must use it right now."

"On you?" Seelios asked.

"There is no one else here, is there?"

Seelios looked down at the ring, its familiar touch against his finger tips. He slipped it on and took a deep breath. The connection was slow and deliberate, not wanting to make any mistakes in his exhausted state. Mana flowed through his body and he felt his mind speak with the ring.

When he opened his eyes, he saw the disciple's energy before him, an amorphous swirling silhouette of blue, gray, and purple almost as dark as a shadow. Deep despair pulled at the disciple's heart, mixing in with an otherwise pure white aura. The visible pain was so intense, Seelios wondered how the man could remain so calm and composed.

Seelios let the connection break, and the image of the disciple's swirling sadness disappeared.

"I . . . I'm sorry, I couldn't continue," Seelios said.

"We are not so different you and I, then, are we?" the disciple said. "We all have our sorrows to bear. I mourn the death of my brother."

Seelios suddenly remembered who the disciple reminded him of.

"Gregory was your brother?" Seelios asked.

The disciple nodded. "He was. I am Ramiel, the last disciple to see you before you receive your judgment."

"I'm so sorry. He saved my life more than once. He was my mentor and my friend, and I would give anything to bring him back." Seelios felt like his heart was crushing inside of his chest.

"I was saddened to hear his fate. The circumstances of his death bring troubling news."

"I don't know why Gameus did what he did."

Ramiel's expression darkened, candlelight dancing around him. "Your mention of the clay men having faces that resembled Raphael, combined with other reports we've received, have lead us to believe that the God of Earth has been creating clay men in the image of the Disciples of Light." Ramiel cleared his throat and straightened up in his seat, visibly disturbed by what he was sharing. "This behavior is quite . . . unusual. He's creating blasphemous visages in mockery of Ophanim. We believe its demonsign."

Seelios felt his heartbeat quicken. Something as horrible as that couldn't be true, but it would explain much. "A god being controlled by a demon? Can that happen?"

"No mortal in this world has ever witnessed or interacted with one. We don't know what's possible and what isn't."

Seelios took a deep breath. "My friend, I think he's been taken by a demon as well."

"We know of Garrick Sandwin. Your relationship with him will factor into your judgment."

"Can you tell me what that means? All the disciples have been coming into this room to ask me questions. Why? What is the judgment for?"

"The disciples have been observing you through questions and their truth rings."

Seelios blinked at this. It was a bit of an obvious statement. "But why? They say I've received training without their permission, but what's the harm in that?"

Ramiel furrowed his brow and his eyes drifted off to the

window. He stared for a few moments before continuing. "The other disciples are . . . concerned of what you might become. Some do not trust your tales of how my brother died and think that you killed him to steal his artifacts for your own purposes."

Seelios balled his fists up and clenched his teeth. He wanted to get up and scream. He wanted to yell so loud that the entire tower could hear him. The chair creaked underneath Seelios as he readjusted himself, taking in several deep breaths to calm himself.

"This was all thrust upon me. I never meant for all those people to die. All I wanted was to save your brother." Seelios locked eyes with Ramiel. "You must believe me."

Ramiel stared back. A silence hung near the length of an eternity as they studied each other. The disciple reached into his robes and pulled out a familiar miniature stone tower topped with a glass marble, and set it down on the table.

"I recognized my brother's totem the moment Mirabelle showed it to me," Ramiel said. "He never did master the art, but still insisted in having one so he could practice. He was the most diligent man I'd ever known."

Ramiel gestured for Seelios to pick it up.

"You're giving it back to me? But, you're his brother. It belongs to you."

A frown spread across Ramiel's face as he looked down at the runic artifact. "No. It was his gift to you and remains yours." He nodded to Seelios's hand. "As is that ring."

Seelios picked up the teleportation totem. He felt mana coursing through its surface, begging to be unleashed. When he used it to save the villagers he'd nearly discharged it to the point of being inert. Now, he held the same artifact with more mana compacted within it than he'd ever thought possible. There was, however, something a bit different about it.

Ramiel stood up from the chair and picked up his candle. "Your judgment will be at the top of the tower today at noon, should you choose to be there." He turned and walked out the door, leaving it wide open behind him.

S eelios got up, walked to the entrance, and watched the candlelight retreat down stone steps that wound out of sight. Every other disciple made it a point to close the door and lock it as they left. It could only mean that Ramiel knew the judgment wouldn't be favorable and wanted him to escape.

An overwhelming sense of dread and frustration came as Seelios grasped the situation that he found himself in. There he was, at the mercy of the protective Disciples of Light, yet in a matter of hours they were going to kill him because he'd been involved in something that he had no choice in.

In mid-thought Seelios heard whispers echoing from up the stair case, punctuated but what he swore was the mention of his own name. He turned his head in the direction of the voices and strained to listen, slowly making his way up the wide stone steps that spiraled along the plain tower wall. Light spilled out of a room with its door half open and Seelios carefully peeked in. Michael and Mirabelle were seated at a table while Anysia paced about on the far side next to a roaring fireplace. Harut leaned against a wall, stroking his beard while lost in a trance of deep concern.

"These reports grow more disturbing by the day," Michael said as he dropped a parchment down on the table, rubbing his eyes in tired resignation. "This senseless violence has no aim. The objectives of the destruction only conflict. Together, they accomplish nothing."

"The demons have no objective, they thrive on chaos and destruction," Anysia said with a stern look.

"These demons have not been seen for millennia," Harut said in his gruff voice, his eyes focused on Anysia. "There's no proof that they've returned. Nothing has changed, the prison remains intact."

"The evidence of demonic presence is all around us. First and foremost the man of Fembleton, right under our watchful nose. What's more, there may be a herald of greed come from the same town." Anysia turned toward the door, causing Seelios to duck behind the wall. He held his breath for a moment, praying he wasn't seen.

"Then why kill so many people?" Michael said. "Nearly every single village between here and the Southern Mountains have been decimated by the God of Earth. If he were possessed then his aim would be to keep those villagers alive. Demons cannot survive without souls to consume and corrupt."

"Then perhaps that is his objective. Perhaps he's not possessed at all and wishes to combat the demons in his own right. Rid the beast of its food and it shall starve," Harut said.

Horror dawned on Seelios at the mention of this. The thought of killing off man just to keep the demons at bay was sickening. What was the point of protecting a defenseless people from evil if there were no more people left to protect.

"I do not think that is his objective," Mirabelle said.

Seelios turned at the sound of the friendly voice and peeked one eye into the room again. Mirabelle sat hunched in her chair, silhouetted by the flames of the fireplace.

"It is my belief he aims for provocation of the gods." Mirabelle lifted the parchment from the table. "These are attacks only on the Paloise kingdom. He wishes to draw the God of Light into action."

"By all that is holy *we* are the God of Light now," Harut said, slamming his fist into his hand with a loud clap. "These people are our charge to protect, yet we sit here and squabble."

Anysia's lip curled up with anger. "You would doom us all! We don't stand a chance against his power. We are bringers of peace and Ophanim's doctrine, not soldiers of war."

"We have someone that can withstand Gameus," Harut stood. "The boy has—"

"Exactly that, a boy!" Anysia yelled. "He is scared and timid, he will fall to the demons before he turns any tide of war. We can't grant more power to one we can't be sure will remain on our side."

Seelios realized he was still clutching the teleportation totem when it began to grow warm in his hand. The light grew bright, causing all conversation in the room to stop. Heads turned in his direction but before any of the disciples could act the light enveloped him and drowned out the world. He'd done nothing to activate it, yet it acted on its own. His feet lifted off into nothingness and he felt his body slip away to some far off place.

He landed on hard packed dirt, kicking up a small cloud

of dust with the planting of his feet. The light faded and he saw the ground he stood on was part of a wide road, rutted deep with wagon tracks. It split the border between a thick tree line and an expansive grass plain. It must've been the Trade Road.

Seelios looked around and saw nothing but unfamiliar trees rustling loudly in the breeze. He wondered how the artifact had brought him there without him even knowing of the place, but then remembered his experience teleporting to the clearing where Emeline died. The sad memory seemed so real that he could smell the blight again.

Seelios gave the air a sniff and realized that it wasn't just a memory, a rotten stench hung in the air that stung his eyes. The trees and vegetation bore no sign of decay, but the smell was coming from somewhere. He turned and followed the scent along the road until he found an opening in the trees. A wooden sign was staked into the ground that said, "Welcome to Pinewood."

Seelios frowned. He'd never been to Pinewood before, or really anywhere near it. He knew of it from travelers' tales and looking at Garrick's atlases, it was one of the largest villages between Fembleton and Paloise, but he'd never traveled so far to actually see it for himself.

He looked down at the artifact. "Why did this thing take me here?"

A path branched off the Trade Road by the sign and into the trees, lined with iron lanterns devoid of flame. The darkness reminded him of the tunnel of dead trees he followed to find his friend and wondered if it was going to be a similar experience. As he walked, a flash of light came from ahead and a wispy wall of luminescence rushed toward him, like a torrential down pour of sunlight surging over the land. Seelios searched for cover, but the wall seemed to stretch out beyond the trees in either direction. Before he could focus on teleporting, the light hit him with a soft warmth and wrapped around him like a down blanket.

Seelios scrambled and kicked, trying to shake off the luminescent film that covered his whole body, clinging to him like a spiderweb. He looked down at his hands and saw the light rippling over his skin, up over his sleeves and clothes. The light moved and flexed with his every movement, covering every square inch of him like a full body suit. When he touched his hands together, he could feel the sensation of pressure, but one hand couldn't feel the other.

He turned back toward Pinewood and noticed that the empty lanterns were now lit with bright wisps, similar to the one Mirabelle had made by Alnerwick. It had to have been the work of a Disciple of Light.

"Hello?" Seelios called out. "Mirabelle? Anysia?" No replies came.

Pinewood was a fishing village with huts and buildings built among the trees instead of a clearing of land like most other villages on Inf. The people didn't believe in deforesting just to make room, they felt they should only take what they need for themselves, which turned out to be very little. Many houses were built around the bases of tree trunks and some up among the branches, connected by drooping bridges of vine and wood.

Seelios looked forward to seeing such a village, and was saddened when he saw the state it was in. As he walked down the path he saw the charred remains of people's homes. Structures in the trees had been ripped down, rope bridges were dangling from branches. Not a soul was in sight.

Up ahead, between a crowded gathering of burnt huts, a light shone through lingering smoke. Squinting his eyes,

Seelios noticed a broad man kneeling down with his hands raised, pleading with someone. When Seelios got closer, he could make out the standing figure of another silhouette, gleaming with an aura of light so bright that it was hard to make out any features. The only thing Seelios could see was a shining armor that looked as reflective as a mirrored surface.

The light disappeared in a flash, along with the armored figure, and the kneeling man was left with his hands outstretched, grasping at nothing. His arms dropped and he slumped to the ground.

Seelios crept closer and the man jumped up, but found his feet unsteady beneath him as if he were weak or exhausted. He braced himself on a thick oak and it turned brown at his touch, its branches sagging. All of its leaves shed at once and blanketed the ground.

Seelios took a step forward, squinting with unsure eyes. "Garrick?"

The man pushed off the tree and took a shaky step. "Seelios, you're here, just like he said." Garrick looked through sunken eyes that held nothing but pain. He still had his wide frame, yet his flesh hung loose on his bones like he suffered from a terrible plague. His skin had turned to a dull gray, with splotches of black all over. The man before Seelios was a shell of his friend, sickly and diseased.

Seelios stepped forward. " I can't believe it's—"

"No, stay back," Garrick said with genuine concern appearing in his eyes. He scanned Seelios up and down, as if he wasn't sure what to make of the light wrapped around his body.

"What happened here? Where are all of the people?" Seelios motioned to their surroundings.

Garrick hugged his arms around his chest, a look of

nervous anxiety about him. "Something horrible is happening to me."

"Garrick, let me help you. The disciples in Paloise, they can heal you. If we just—"

"No!" Garrick yelled, causing Seelios to jump back involuntarily. "It's too late for me. I must to tell you something."

"Whatever it may be, tell me in Paloise." Seelios held out the teleportation totem. "I can use this to take us there in an instant."

Garrick shook his head. "Please, you must listen. I have little time left." He contorted in pain, snapping his head back as he let out a scream. Seelios noticed the shimmering crystal that hung from his friend's neck.

Garrick thrashed his head about and began flailing his arms wildly as if he were fighting off something, and losing. He fell to the ground and grazed a bush that retracted from his touch, disintegrating into a pile of wilt.

"What's happening to you?" Seelios asked, terror in his eyes.

"Gods, why didn't he help me. He could've ended it," Garrick whispered to himself. He lifted his eyes to Seelios. "I have only a small amount of time to speak with you. Soon, the demon will take me back." Garrick winced in pain, he clutched his chest with one hand. "You must stop them."

Garrick fell down to his knees and screamed again, shutting his eyes in pain.

"Who?" Seelios asked, but Garrick didn't answer as he fell to his side and curled up into a fetal position.

Still laying on the ground, he lifted a single finger up towards the sky. At first, Seelios wasn't sure what he was pointing at. He searched the tree tops for someone or something to be looking down on them, but saw nothing but empty branches and abandoned huts. Beyond the treetops the Daylight Star twinkled in the sky as bright as ever.

"The demons. They are growing stronger," Garrick said through raspy breaths. "They've taken control of me and others too. Soon they will walk upon the earth."

"The gods will stop them," Seelios said, looking back down at his friend.

Garrick seized with pain for a moment, then gave a small chuckle. "The gods have no idea what they've done, imprisoning them in the sky of the mortal realm. I've seen it with my own eyes. Their power is terrible, growing stronger every day. The gods will be powerless against them." He lifted his head, his eyes black as midnight. Something else other than his friend peered back at Seelios.

Seelios activated his truth ring and felt the mana creep into his vision. A small circle of yellow light in Garrick's chest was shrinking fast against a sea of darkness. Blackness oozed out of his aura, curling up to the sky.

"Go, get out of here," Garrick said through gritted teeth. "You need to leave." He gave one final blood-curdling scream as the light in his chest winked out of existence. In that same moment, a wave of ashen decay spread out from where he lay. It rippled out to the surrounding trees and swept up their trunks. Life drained from their limbs as the colors of green were replaced with brown and black. Huts and wooden planks from walkways crashed to the ground as the branches grew too weak to support the weight.

Seelios stepped back, watching the forest around him bow down in submission to the plague that spread from Garrick. Witnessing such destruction of life, Seelios knew it had to be true. For the first time in the existence of humanity, the demons were among them.

The plague rushed up to his feet and the barrier of light

flickered and flashed with blinding intensity. Rotting earth surrounded him on all sides and the decay tried to slide up around his ankles. Seelios looked down at his hands and saw the color of his skin through tiny holes in the golden light as the barrier struggled to hold together.

Not wanting to see what would happen if the plague overtook him, Seelios activated the teleportation totem.

WHEN THE LIGHT FADED, Seelios wasn't sure where he'd find himself. The artifact, while working on his command, seemed to be operating independently. He didn't have a place in mind when he was whisked away, yet he found his landing surprisingly graceful. His feet touched down on soft tufts of grass. When his surroundings came into view, he saw the tops of trees stretching in all directions. He spun to see Paloise's walls and turrets far away.

Seelios thought about Garrick's words. Demonic possession and voices of temptation were supposed to be nothing but myth. The tales Seelios had read were so unimaginably horrific that it seemed impossible to be anything more than just a story. But what happened to Garrick, that was real, and if everything else he said was true then more will bend to the demons' will.

The sun was nearing its highest point in the sky, almost noon. Seelios looked toward Paloise and activated his ring. The shimmering stone of Ophanim's Grand Temple appeared like a glowing beacon, stretching up into the clouds. The light he saw in Pinewood, the protective barrier, the other figure; it all must've meant that one of the disciples was there. He had to go to find answers.

The light of the totem took him once more, but this time he knew his destination with purpose. When the light faded, blue skies dotted with white clouds stretched in every direction. He turned and all of the disciples were gathered in a semi-circle, standing in between the pillars around the outside perimeter of the stone platform. They stared at him in silence, wearing looks that seemed to resemble something close to reverence.

"One of you was there!" Seelios yelled. "Someone could've helped him, but you just let him suffer. I thought you were supposed to protect people."

The disciples continued to regard him in silence. Seelios glanced around, frustration beginning to build.

"Which one of you was it? Or was it all of you?" Seelios said.

A radiant light came from behind Seelios, casting a long shadow from his feet that stretched out to the other side of the platform.

"It was me," a familiar voice said. A voice that Seelios had known his entire life. One that spoke with conviction and wisdom.

Seelios turned and looked at the man standing behind him. "F—father?"

Ricker stood before him in brilliant armor that shone like a mirror. A white cape draped over his pauldrons and hung with regal grace behind him. His eyes glowed with a white radiance that could only come from a true god.

"My son," Ricker said. "You've had to go through so much. I'm so sorry."

"Lord Ophanim, you've regained your power!" Ramiel said with surprise and excitement in his voice.

Seelios turned and saw all of the disciples had dropped down to one knee, stealing looks up at Ricker, awestruck.

"Not all of it," Ricker said to the disciple, then turned back to Seelios. "I'm glad Gregory was able to save you from

Fembleton, he will be missed more than you know. What Gameus did, it was—"

"You've been a god this whole time? *The* god of our realm?" Seelios raised his voice. "Where were you when all those people died?"

"You will stay your tongue when our lord is before you, boy," Raphael said as he stood.

Ricker held up his hand. "He has every right to be angry. I've kept much from him."

"Garrick is suffering, father. You were there, you saw him. Why didn't you help him?"

"I tried. Garrick is beyond mine or anyone else's power here to help. All but perhaps one," Ricker said, fixing his eyes on Seelios. A wind whipped over the platform, sending Ricker's cape swirling about him.

"Why . . . why are you doing this to me? Why have you put me through all this?" Seelios said, dropping his eyes to the ground.

"My lord, the boy is not of sound spirit. He has too much inner turmoil," Anysia said from the far edge of the platform.

"Were you or anyone else here that much different?" Ricker said to the disciples. They glanced at each other in silence.

"Why is this happening?" Seelios whispered.

"It saddens me that you were born into a world on the brink of darkness," Ricker said. "But with you, there's a chance to save it. You have a power within you."

Seelios saw the ruins of Fembleton in his mind, his hometown destroyed before him. He saw the deaths of all the people who died in Alnerwick. He saw the pain on Garrick's face. If there was even a possibility to keep any more of that from happening, he had to try.

"Seelios. Mortals need our help, but we can't do it alone. We need you with us," Ricker said. "Will you join us?"

Seelios looked at his father. He stared into the glowing eyes of the God of Light, his father, and he saw in them something that he'd never seen before in his life: pride.

"I will," Seelios said.

ABOUT THE AUTHOR

David is a federal consultant and part-time writer originally from Middletown, Maryland. He's crafted fantasy stories pulling from literary, cinematic, and video gaming epiphanies that every 90s kid experienced in front of their living room TV. Unless that kid didn't have cable, like David. His passion to submerge the reader into worlds wrought with strife and wonder drives him to create fresh stories and original narratives. Please visit his social media pages and subscribe to the newsletter for the latest updates on his work.

www.david-chesney.com
contact@david-chesney.com

54920808R00128

Made in the USA
Middletown, DE
07 December 2017